MW01051128

THE TIME OF HIS LIFE?

One by one the tourists were introduced to the President. Abraham Lincoln's grip was incredibly strong. Rafe knew they needed a reason for petitioning an audience with Lincoln, and had already worked out their story.

Unfortunately, he didn't have time to use it.

Marden was trembling as the President extended his hand. "The Ford's Theater," Marden stammered. "John Wilkes Booth has said that he intends to shoot you. He must be stopped!"

"I see," Lincoln said. He stepped back, lowering his hand. "You have done your duty well. One of my aides may have a few questions for you, before you leave."

Rafe was stunned. "We have to get out of here," he whispered. *"Go!"*

Books in the Robert Silverberg's Time Tours *series*

Robert Silverberg's
Time Tours

GLORY'S END

by
Nick Baron

A Byron Preiss Book

HarperPaperbacks
A Division of HarperCollins*Publishers*

This novel is dedicated to
Scott Ciencin
with thanks and appreciation.

This is a work of fiction. The characters, incidents, and
dialogues are products of the author's imagination and
are not to be construed as real. Any resemblance to
actual events or persons, living or dead, is entirely
coincidental.

HarperPaperbacks A Division of HarperCollins*Publishers*
10 East 53rd Street, New York, N.Y. 10022

Text and artwork copyright © 1990 by Byron Preiss
Visual Publications, Inc.
Afterword copyright © 1990 Agberg, Ltd.

All rights reserved. No part of this book may be used or
reproduced in any manner whatsoever without written
permission of the publisher, except in the case of brief
quotations embodied in critical articles and reviews.
For information, address HarperCollins*Publishers*
10 East 53rd Street, New York, N.Y. 10022

Cover painting by Kevin Johnson
Interior illustrations by Alex Niño
Edited by John Betancourt
Logo and cover design by Fleming Hays Group, Inc.
Book design by Michael Goode
Special thanks to Ricia Mainhardt, Dan Weiss, Susan
Kitzen, and Chris Fortunato.

First printing: December 1990
Printed in the United States of America

HarperPaperbacks and colophon are trademarks of
HarperCollins*Publishers*

10 9 8 7 6 5 4 3 2 1

Dear Time Traveler,

You have entered the now-time year of 2061.
When time travel was discovered, fifty or so
years before, the powers-that-be decided to make
time traveling a tourist business. After all, you
can't have people wandering around on their own,
changing history—think of the effect on the future!

To begin, you must sign up for a tour at one
of the Time Tour Travel Stations. Which tour do
you want? The Roman Empire? The U.S. Civil
War? The Prehistoric Era?

After you choose, you're outfitted in the
appropriate costume of the era. Next you're given
a hypno-sleep course in whatever language you
may need. Finally you snap on your Time Belt
and meet the Time Courier, who'll lead your tour.

The courier wears the Master Belt, which
controls your belt. So don't go try jimmying
your mechanism and slipping away . . .

What happens if you do? Well, there's an
organization known as the Time Patrol to police
such things. And if they catch a tourist or Courier
monkeying around with the past, the penalty is
swift *and* permanent. They may edit *you* out
of history.

So have fun . . . and be careful.

Time Service Management

Chapter One
CHANCELLORSVILLE, VIRGINIA, MAY 2, 1863

Ashell exploded to the left of the young, dark-haired man, and a blinding white flash seared the darkness. The Time Courier felt a wave of force push at him. Artillery fire thundered from the woods, and shrapnel littered the road ahead.

Rafe Williamson was terrified. Stepping over the body of a soldier as another shell struck the road behind him, the seventeen-year-old Courier thought, *He's not much older than I am.*

Ahead, several men in gray uniforms carried the wounded General Stonewall Jackson. Barely a hundred meters separated the young man and the soldiers. The soldiers set their burden down and ran for the shelter of the thickets. A preacher stayed behind.

As the young Courier watched, two musket balls whistled over his head. He dove to the side as grape-shot struck sparks on the flint-like rocks where he had been standing a moment before.

Rafe covered his head as lead shot, horseshoe nails, and small stones blasted overhead with frightening velocity. Lying in the midst of the chaos, he wondered if the man he was trying to protect deserved his efforts. He had risked his job by not notifying the Time Patrol.

There were two main branches of the Time Service: the Time Couriers, who escorted tourists through carefully supervised visits to the past, and the Time Patrol, whose function was to protect the sanctity of twenty-first century now-time at all costs. Rafe worked as a Time Courier, specializing in the American Civil War. His record showed dozens of successful and highly praised tours through those fateful years.

This tour was not destined to be one of them.

George Coffin, one of his tourists, had assumed the place of Reverend James Power Smith and was about to commit a timecrime of major proportions. Continuing to look through the Infra-ready glasses, Rafe glimpsed Stonewall Jackson's heavily bearded face. Jackson's dark hair had been combed back to reveal a proud forehead, now scratched and bloody. His intense dark eyes were aflame with pain and determination.

Coffin leaned over the general. He held a vial filled with white tablets in one hand.

Penicillin tablets, Rafe deduced. Jackson was fated to live for several more days before succumbing to pleurisy and pneumonia at 3:13 P.M. on May 10, 1863. With Coffin's medication, the general had a fighting chance to live and perhaps command again, despite the loss of his arm. The South might win the Civil War.

Rafe used his Master Belt to shunt up the line.

Suddenly it was several days before the battle, and the woods were quiet. The terror and confusion of the nighttime battle had been replaced by the peace of a sunny Virginia afternoon. Rafe walked back to the open field a mile west of Chancellorsville and spotted the old cabin where he had left—would leave—his charges several days in the future.

Failing to report a potential timecrime was a violation of the Time Service's rules. Rafe's tour group was sizeable, a dozen tourists and himself, and the tour had proceeded without a hitch for its first five days. He had missed any warning signs that Coffin was about to commit a timecrime. Coffin had been up the line to the Glory Road, as the Time Service's marketing division called the Civil War, several times before, twice with Rafe as Courier. There had been no indication of instability. Rafe assumed he was a no-risk tourist.

Coffin's disappearance had happened quickly. One moment he was there, off to the back of the tour group; the next, he was gone. Rafe's options had been limited: summon the Time Patrol or go after the runaway himself. Rafe chased after Coffin.

Rafe didn't worry about leaving his tourists unattended; if he spent half a lifetime tracking down his rogue tourist, he could always set his timer so as to return to the rest of the group after only minutes or seconds had passed in their objective reality.

It had taken hours for him to pick up Coffin's trail, which led him to the present moment.

Assuming a position where he would be able to observe his tour group from their rear, his back against the cabin, Rafe set his Time Belt and shunted.

The afternoon vanished, suddenly replaced by twilight. His tour group was there, off to the left side of the cabin, near the front. This was the point where it became tricky, because a dark-haired, green-eyed, and moderately handsome young Time Courier named Rafe Williamson was still there as well.

Rafe stared at his past-self and swallowed hard.

He had shunted down the line to the time before Coffin sneaked off; it was imperative that his past-self did not become aware of his now-self's presence. Meeting yourself was a timecrime of the highest order and carried a severe punishment.

His group had witnessed the shooting of General Jackson, then shunted back to an earlier time when the area was clear of fighting. After walking back to the clearing, they shunted forward to watch Brigadier General Robert E. Rodes and his staff gather their troops.

Coffin broke away from the others. When the auburn-haired deserter turned the corner and found Rafe waiting, he opened his mouth in surprise.

Rafe slammed the man against the wall.

"Stay quiet," Rafe whispered. "I know where you're going, and I know what you're planning to do. It'll never work."

He fished through Coffin's pockets.

"I don't know what you're talking—"

The vial of tablets was in Rafe's hand before Coffin could finish his denial. Coffin blanched as the young Time Courier ran through the events he had witnessed.

Suddenly sounds of confusion and excitement issued from the tour group. Rafe's past-self had noticed Coffin's absence and was coming their way. Rafe grabbed Coffin and pulled him around the cabin, then peaked around the corner to see his past-self go in search of the deserter.

After confiscating the penicillin tablets and delivering a stiff warning about what the Time Patrol did to misguided tourists, Rafe brought Coffin back to the group.

Unfortunately, there was still one problem: What about the other Rafe Williamson, the one who had gone off in search of Coffin and would now never find him? Rafe had allowed himself to become a victim of the Paradox of Duplication.

There was only one way to get out of the situation. Rafe drafted a detailed letter and found a boy from the drummer corps who would act as a messenger.

"The man you're looking for is my brother," Rafe said. "We're twins. We even dress exactly alike. He answers to the name Rafe Williamson. I expect he'll be back this way shortly."

Rafe shunted his group to the next event on the tour. Just before the he brought the group to their new observation post, a messenger arrived with a letter from the other Rafe Williamson.

"I understand and will comply," it read. "Time travel is pretty weird, huh? R.W."

Rafe felt relieved. His letter had instructed the other Rafe to proceed to the exact location where he found Coffin with Stonewall Jackson. Then the other Rafe was to shunt to the exact same instant that he had shunted to. As no two bodies that had once been one could occupy the same physical and temporal location, the two lives would merge.

The second Rafe had not returned to the group. Rafe's efforts had been successful. The second Rafe had joined with the first. The problem was solved.

The tour proceeded fairly smoothly from that point on, though Coffin was sullen much of the time.

The vial of tablets in Rafe's pocket became a heavy weight as the days went on. On the last day of the tour, Rafe tried to make peace with Coffin. The tourist glared at the Courier and walked away from Rafe's outstretched hand without a word.

This trip up the line hadn't been much fun. But if Rafe had known all the trouble that would be waiting for him back down the line, he might have stayed in the past.

There were several positions in the Time Service less glamorous than serving as a Time Courier or a Time Patrolman. Working the front desk was one. The Time Service was short-handed, and Time Couriers like Rafe had been forced to pitch in.

Rafe didn't mind. His two-week layover had ended the day before, and his cruise on the Civil War ironclad warship, the U.S.S. *Monitor*, had been exactly the distraction he needed.

The morning passed quickly, if not pleasantly. Rafe maintained his good mood, despite having to explain to a tourist and his friends why the tourist would not be permitted on a tour he had sponsored. There was some minor mischief he would commit if he were allowed to go.

"You see, Mr. Grundrekker, for us your tour is a matter of recorded fact. The other members of your group are free to continue. But the best I can offer you is a refund."

The tourist would not budge. Finally Rafe played a holo supplied by the Time Patrol.

"I said *that* to the Queen of England?"

Rafe nodded. "Yes. See the angry-looking people with the swords? This is not good. Trust me."

Grundrekker accepted his refund.

After watching the clock for another hour, Rafe cleaned up for the Courier scheduled to relieve him. He was on his feet, gathering his files, when the hydraulic doors hissed open and a beautiful dark-haired girl emerged.

She looked about the same age as Rafe, with bright green eyes and a daring smile. A synth-leather compression pack was slung over her shoulder, and a gray envelope was in her hand. She wore a jade-green top with billowing sleeves ending in alumifoil cuffs. A thin white belt was laced into her black leather pantalettes, which ended just above the knees.

Their eyes locked. The girl's body tensed, her shoulders drew tight. She raised her chin slightly, and her smile vanished.

Rafe silently formed her name: Denise.

She didn't leave. One hand nervously played over the delicate hollow at the base of her throat, where her neck muscles converged in a perfect V. Denise moved forward and stopped before him.

"You look good, Rafe," she said softly.

His heart stopped dead for a moment. He had been angry, then hurt, then resigned for months after their breakup. He had dated a dozen girls since then, but it had never been the same. At the university, he tried to bury himself in his studies. His grades had improved, but that didn't help his pain. Only the Time Service had offered a true escape.

As he looked across the desk at her soft, creamy skin and delicate features, he was startled to realize that despite it all, he still loved her.

Denise sat down on the web in front of the desk, her fingers absently climbing to the underside of her chin. "I didn't know you'd be here. I'm working at the Under D.C. Museum until next semester. Studying art history, you know. You're still an artist, aren't you?"

"It's a hobby. This is my third summer as a Courier. I do the Civil War years."

"That's right. You had an ancestor who was a major in the Confederacy."

Plugging in the desk holo, Rafe placed his thumb on the command screen. "Gettysburg."

In response to his command, the battle erupted in full force on top of his desk. Denise jumped back, startled.

"End run," Rafe instructed the machine, and the battle vanished. "Sorry. I didn't mean to scare you."

"You didn't," she said. But her face was pale as she handed the gray envelope to Rafe. "I'm going on a tour. Maybe you can tell me where to find registration and wardrobe?"

He was amazed at how painfully ordinary and reserved their conversation was. How polite. Even so, she had trouble maintaining eye contact, and shifted frequently in her chair.

Rafe was about to open the envelope to see what tour Denise had booked, when the door behind Rafe's desk hissed open and his replacement appeared.

"Pendergrass wants to see you right away," the other Courier croaked. "It's not good."

Rafe looked back to Denise and placed her envelope on the desk. He knew it would be best for both of them if he simply walked away.

"Mr. Halberstam will call one of the servo-bots to help you, Ms. Chillington," he said.

Chapter Three

"**M**y boy," Ivan Pendergrass said, the words oozing from the man like the sweat that covered his face. "So glad you could make it."

The general manager of the Under Washington, D.C., branch of the Time Service was immense, a mountain of a man. He wore a Mayan headdress to cover his balding head, and neo-gold chains to hide his hairless chest. An authentic twentieth-century Hawaiian shirt, accentuated his timeless lack of taste. A chaotic whirl of paraphernalia from across time filled his office.

The tips of Pendergrass's fat, stubby fingers ground together. The blood drained from his fingernails, turning them white.

"I like you, boy. I remember when you first came here looking for a job. I was the one that hired you. You remember that, Rafe?"

The young Courier nodded. He had been 15,

the youngest applicant ever accepted into the Time Service.

"I won't lie to you, son. You had credentials, and it was a great P.R. move. Kids just love to see someone their own age bossing adults around. But everyone has to grow up sometime. I understand you graduated from the university this year. You majored in bio-engineering."

"And minored in Art History. That's right."

"I'd like you to have a nice, long, prosperous future with the Service and avoid minor annoyances like criminal charges—but you seem determined to muck that all up!"

"Coffin," Rafe muttered. The man had talked.

"He asked for a refund. We asked why, and he wouldn't say. Just that he was unhappy with the tour. So we sent someone back to monitor your tour, and she saw the whole thing."

Rafe sunk into the plush chair. "So I'm fired?"

"You're on probation. Another Courier will monitor your actions on the tour you have leaving this afternoon. He'll make a report, and we'll take it from there." The fat man smiled unnervingly. "I view you as an asset. That's why I'm willing to give you a second chance. But if there are any more screwups, I'll have no choice but to terminate your employment. I hope I've made myself clear."

"Yes, sir," Rafe said. He felt horrible, but he refused to let it show. "I have some changes to the

Glory Road tour that I want to go over with you," he added.

"At your discretion, boy. Just keep it safe and interesting." Pendergrass lowered his gaze and said warmly, "I trust you."

Chapter Four

Several hours later, Rafe's tour group sat impatiently in the briefing room. Two members of the group were missing; the Courier assigned as his probation officer, and one of the tourists. Rafe decided to have the lost tourist paged. When he checked the roster and learned Denise was the missing tourist, his heart sank. Rafe called Data Central to deliver the page.

Rafe surveyed his tourists as he waited. They had already been to the wardrobe department and were wearing their period costumes. Only one, a tall, gaunt historian named William Marden, seemed at all comfortable with his new change of clothing. When Rafe complimented Marden, the man simply sneered and said, "I'm a recreation costumer. I wore these clothes over here. Even my spectacles are authentic!"

Rafe excused himself. Approaching a group of

two adults and two teenagers standing near the emergency exit, Rafe held out his hand and forced a smile.

"Good afternoon! You must be the Stuart family. I'm Rafe Williamson, your Courier."

Jack Stuart took Rafe's hand in a tight grip and nodded. He was a handsome man in his late thirties with thinning blond hair and an excellent physique.

"Pleased to meet you," he said. "This is my wife, Margot."

"Your parents must be so proud of you," Margot said as she laid her hand on Rafe's shoulder. She was an attractive brunette, also in her late thirties, with a figure that a artist would have had difficulty improving. Her hands were very cold, and her eyes were sad, despite the smile she maintained at all times.

"Um, yes. Yes, they are," Rafe said. *Actually, they think I'm crazy.*

"And this is my son, Chuck, and my daughter, Kyla."

Chuck moved first, cutting off his sister. His gray-blue eyes lit up, and the veins in his massive neck surged as he shook Rafe's hand. Rafe could tell that Chuck's athletic build had nothing to do with sports. Even at sixteen, he had the glazed look of a holo-vid addict.

"I've seen you on the holo-vid," Chuck said, "during the state reduced-gravity Jai-Lai championships on the Extra-Sensory Sports Network. You went one-on-one with Zero Deville!"

"And I lost, just like everyone else that got paired up with him." Rafe laughed.

"Don't mind him," Kyla said as she brushed past Chuck. She had long blond hair and deep blue eyes. Her lips and cheeks were rosy, and her billowing period dress couldn't hide the figure she had inherited from her mother. "I think it's very brave that you made the effort." She took Rafe's hand in both of hers and winked. "I would have been in your class if you had gone to the local. I've heard all about you. I suppose working as a Courier must be very rewarding. You must have all sorts of adventures."

Suddenly she frowned. She winked several times, and the perfect blue of her left eye seemed to slip. "Stupid contact lens!"

Without warning, she turned and stomped off to the ladies' room. Margot set off after her daughter.

"Just what we need, a sports hero!"

Rafe spun and found himself eye-to-eye with fifteen-year-old Tarrant Thurlow. Tarrant had a pleasing face now twisted in a sneer.

"You must be—" Rafe began.

"Save it for someone who's planning on leaving you a tip, loser."

Tarrant located a web in the corner of the room and deposited himself.

"Okay," Rafe said. Then the main doors hissed open, and Denise entered, shepherded by a pudgy man in his mid-forties. She avoided eye contact with Rafe and gravitated toward the Stuarts. The pudgy man approached Rafe and slapped a holo-cube in his hand.

"That's my authorization. Want to view it?"

Rafe hesitated. "And you are?"

The man shook his head and engaged the viewer. The image of a familiar Mayan headdress popped into the air. "Rafe, this is D. W. Carollan. He's your probation officer. If you screw up, it's his job to document it." The image of Pendergrass leaned forward. "Look Rafe, he's kind of a nertz—"

The phantom Pendergrass vanished as Carollan snatched the holo-cube.

Rafe saw that the entire tour group had focused on the holo. Even Denise seemed worried.

"That was supposed to be a private message!" Rafe hissed.

Carollan cleared his throat and turned to address the tourists.

Rafe got there first. "There's no reason for any of you to be upset. This is just a routine check. Isn't that right, D.W.?"

"Well, no."

"Can I talk to you for a moment? In private?"

Carollan wrinkled his nose and withdrew his pocket holo-notation device. "A proposal to violate the first law, never leave the tour group by themselves," he said into the device.

"That's only when we're up the line!" Rafe protested.

Carollan frowned and clicked on the machine to instruct, "Scratch that."

"Will you come with me?" Rafe snarled.

In the hallway outside, Rafe said, "Do you know what you just did?"

"My actions are above reproach."

"You just compromised my authority in front of

the tourists. Their lives may depend on following my orders without a second's hesitation, and you've just given them a reason not to trust me."

"You're exaggerating, of course," D.W. said mildly.

Rafe rubbed his forehead. "I don't understand this. I thought I knew every time Courier in Under D.C. Did they transfer you from another branch?"

"No," Carollan said. "I've been a teacher at this facility for fifteen years, Mr. Williamson!"

Rafe shook his head. He wanted to asked Carollan how extensive his field training had been, but he knew better.

The instructor suddenly patted Rafe on the shoulder. In a booming, confident classroom voice, he said, "And just call me Dewey, all right?"

"Sure," Rafe said, fighting back his surprise at the instructor's sudden turnaround. An instant later, he was confronting the reason for Dewey's abrupt attitude change.

"Thomas Craig Petric, Lieutenant First Class, Time Patrol," the man said. The Patrolman stood at about a hundred and seventy centimeters and his gray uniform was cut to accentuate his perfect physique. He had black hair, a thick black mustache, and beady gray eyes.

The young Courier instinctively took a step back and almost tripped on Dewey. The instructor had somehow maneuvered behind him.

Petric flashed his perfect smile. "No need for alarm, gentlemen. I understand you have a tour that's preparing to depart shortly?"

Rafe nodded. "The Glory Road tour is about to

begin. The tourists are inside, waiting to be briefed."

"Excellent. I'd like to come along. That is, provided neither of you has any objections."

Dewey said, "Objections? Of course not! In fact, let me be the first to welcome you to our little tour!"

"Hold it," Rafe said. "Why this tour?"

Petric shrugged. "You're the next one out. But you're right, I owe you some explanation."

In truth, a Patrolman owed a Courier absolutely nothing, and Rafe knew it. Anything Petric chose to tell them was a professional courtesy, nothing more.

"A counterfeiting ring has been attempting to alter history by unbalancing the economies of several eras. Tours have been chosen at random for close scrutiny. You people just happened to be at the right place at the right time."

"Story of my life," Rafe muttered.

"I have to check in with wardrobe and get suited up. You'll introduce me as a late addition to the tour, nothing else. Is that clear?"

Dewey swallowed hard. "Yes," he said in a tiny voice.

Chapter Five

"**O**kay, let's go over it one more time," Rafe said to the assembled tourists. "What is your primary concern while you're in the past? Tarrant?"

The boy had been rocking back and forth silently in his web since the briefing began. He tried to blow a few strands of blond of hair away from his eyes. "Don't leave any biodegradables?"

"Party till you drop!" Chuck added gleefully. "I learned that one in history this week."

"No," Rafe said softly. "Safety. Your primary concern is *safety*."

Dewey stood up and stepped in front of the young Courier. Rafe sighed as Dewey said, "People, people, it's simple. Keep your head low, do not engage the natives unless you have permission from us to do so, don't try to take anything back with you that's not on the list I'll pass out, and don't muck around with history. Is everyone clear on that?"

There was a chorus of grunts in the affirmative. Dewey turned back to Rafe. "Anything you wish to add?"

"Not really."

"Good. Then help me distribute this list of dos and don'ts, and we'll be on our way."

As the tourists were studying Dewey's lists, Petric arrived, and Rafe introduced him as a professor of neo-zoology on a sabbatical. Petric hesitated when he was introduced to the Stuart family, tapping his fingers against his lips. "Stuart. Margot Stuart. Aha!"

Rafe got nervous whenever he heard a Patrolman say that.

"I've read one of your books, haven't I?"

Margot shifted uncomfortably. "I don't know. Have you?"

"Of course. *Women Who Loathe Men and the Men Who Love Them* Twenty-nine weeks on the bestseller list."

Margot's eyelashes fluttered. "It's nothing really."

Dewey took a quick head-count and said, "Gentlemen and ladies, let's set our timers!"

Rafe had already explained to the tourists that the timers on their Time Belts were controlled by the timer in his Master Belt. Now, tapping the instructor on the shoulder, Rafe took Dewey to the side and said quietly, "If we shunt from here, we'll materialize in solid rock. We have to go upworld and take a pod first."

"Don't you think I know that?" Dewey said unconvincingly.

Just then, Petric went up to the two men and

said, "Excuse me, just who's running this tour, anyway?"

The instructor blanched and pointed at Rafe. "He is!"

The Patrolman's eyes narrowed to slits. "Great. Then let him do his job. I don't know about the rest of your tourists, but I don't like to be kept waiting. . . ."

Chapter Six

Kyla had been doing her best to get Rafe's attention throughout the long pod-ride. She had crossed and uncrossed her legs several times, batted her eyelashes, attempted to be coy, done her best to be blatant—and failed to raise much more than a professional smile from the young Courier. When she finally understood that her attentions were being wasted on Rafe, she became frustrated.

Just as she had done for most of her life, she targeted her brother, Chuck. At the moment, she was calling him a polymorph, a human lump who maintains a near-perfect physique without doing a wit of exercise. Then she called him a mental polymorph, a human lump without an ounce of brains who somehow manages to walk upright and breathe at the same time.

"You know, you're going to have to dress like a man when we get to Gettysburg," Chuck said mildly.

"Rafe said you'll look good with facial hair, that it would be an improvement."

Kyla turned white. She was about to switch from verbal to physical abuse when her father interceded.

"Don't mind them," Jack Stuart said to Rafe as he moved forward and clamped his hands on his children's shoulders. "I'm sure the little *sweethearts* are just suffering from podlag."

The journey to Maryland *had* been bumpy so far. The east coast pod maintenance contract had been won by a new firm, and the transitional period had not been smooth. Nevertheless, the pod had arrived on time, and their aerotaxi was waiting. Dinner was served on the puddle jumper, and twilight approached as the aerotaxi flew over the Maryland border.

The taxi landed at the Antietam Battlefield park just before nightfall, and Rafe took the group to the remains of the Nicodemus farmhouse. Of the barn outside the farmhouse, only the north wall remained, a lone sentinel guarding a field that had once yielded a healthy crop of corn. Rafe set his timer.

"You're about to see the approach of nine thousand Union soldiers as they meet the Confederates. Remember—"

"*Don't talk with anybody!*" the tourists shouted.

The Courier said softly, "You're about to become a part of history," then pressed the timer on his Master Belt.

Chapter Seven
ANTIETAM, MARYLAND, SEPTEMBER 17, 1862

A small field stood beyond the barn. Hagerstown Turnpike, a dirt road, lay ahead. Across the road lay the Millers' forty-acre cornfield. The air was hot and musty. The unfamiliar smells of hay and livestock came from inside the barn.

The sky was steel-gray, and a fine mist clung to the cornfield. Lines of soldiers marched past to the beat of company drummers. Artillery fire blazed, and shells whistled through the air and exploded.

Only a half-dozen people were present in the farmhouse when the tourists appeared. Their backs were turned, and they didn't notice the group's sudden materialization. The basement doors were open, and the people were scurrying down the steps. Rafe and his tourists joined those seeking refuge.

A gray-eyed, wild-haired man in his forties turned to the tourists as they raced down the stairs, into the shadowy cellar. Two men, a woman, and two children stood just behind him. Another man stood near one of the basement windows, looking out toward the cornfield. Rafe guessed that the stern-looking man before him was the farmer Nicodemus.

"Who are you folks?"

"We was on our way to Shepardstown," Rafe said earnestly. "The Union soldiers said we'd never make it. They said we could take refuge here. We weren't plannin' on it, really. We just got no place else to go."

"What's that in your hands?"

"My sketchpad. I do drawings and sell 'em to the magazines sometimes. I'm real good. In fact, I got this letter here from *Harper's Weekly*. Wanna see?"

Beyond the group, the man at window turned slightly at this, then looked back to the cornfield.

"These folks is my family from—"

There was a shocking burst of sound as mortar fire struck the barn.

The gray-eyed man turned away. "Just don't be takin' none of our food. The soldiers didn't leave us much, an' we gotta make it last after they're gone."

"No sir. Hungry, we ain't. Just tired and scared."

The man went back to his family and ignored the group.

"Okay," Rafe said as he brought the tourists to one of the shoulder-height windows. When he was sure no one was looking, he fastened several sheets of protective latexsteel to the glass.

The tourists crowded around as Rafe tapped his ear. Then the tourists put their hands to their heads, as if their ears were ringing. In truth, they were all activating the privacy ear implants, called Ears, given to them during their physicals.

Unknown to everyone but Rafe, the Ears also served another purpose: Inside their microcircuitry was an alarm sensor programed to alert the young Courier if any of his tourists moved more than four meters from the group.

"Can everyone hear me loud and clear?" Rafe whispered.

There was a chorus of affirmative grunts.

"On September fifth, the Confederate Army crossed the Potomac in a desperate move to invade the North. The Southern armies and cities needed supplies if they were going to endure. The Virginia farmlands had been devastated by the war, but the Northern fields were practically untouched.

"Also, Europe was leaning toward support of the Rebel army. A major victory at this stage might have secured their assistance in the war effort. But Lee did not anticipate the swift and terrible response by McClellan, leader of the Union army.

"On September twelfth, after the Union victory in Fredrick, young private Mitchell and another Union soldier from the Twenty-seventh Indiana Infantry were resting in a field that had recently housed Lee's headquarters. They found a rare bounty, three cigars wrapped in paper. On that paper were written the words 'Headquarters, Army of Northern Virginia.'

"This was a copy of Lee's Special Order number one ninety-one, which detailed Lee's plan of attack. By giving his sergeant, John Bloss, that note, Mitchell sealed the man's death warrant. The sergeant was killed in McClellan's counterassault.

"Outside this window, you will see the further results of that chance discovery. But first, let's review what you learned in hypno-sleep. A regiment consists of one thousand and forty-six men. Four regiments comprise a brigade. Three brigades form a division. Three divisions make a corps. That's over thirty-seven *thousand* brave young men per corps."

The tourists strained to peek out the basement windows. The far right flank of the first corps was sweeping through the farmhouse yard. Marching from the north, double lines of soldiers approached like a slow-moving blue tide. They charged, battle flags forward, the regulation flag of their state and the Union flag snapping fiercely above their heads. Every stalk of corn fell in the first great blaze of gunfire. Men fell just as fast. The forty-acre cornfield played host to a holocaust as the area changed hands ten times over the course of the morning.

"You're about to see the Iron Brigade, one of the few units to actually receive a name, enter the battle. Remember your history, and think of these boys as the Green Berets and the Eighty-second Airborne rolled into one elite strike force. These soldiers were nicknamed 'them damn black-hat boys' for the distinctive headgear they all wore, a huge black-crowned hat with a wide brim, one side turned up with a plume in it."

"This is fascinating," Jack Stuart said. "Like walking through a living, breathing museum."

Rafe would have preferred shunting to the highlights of the morning, allowing the tourists to witness the entire movement in minutes instead of hours, but he could not have his group appearing and disappearing in front of the natives.

The morning passed quickly, with Rafe pointing out the important details: "There you see John B. Hood's Texas Brigade fighting with the fury of the devil, enraged because their first decent meal in days has been interrupted.

"Here you have a perfect view of the Federals' six-gun battery, used to tear apart the charge of the Texans. The intense fighting you are witnessing this morning has been regarded as some of the bloodiest and most fierce of the war.

"Despite outnumbering Lee's army eighty-seven thousand to forty-one thousand, McClellan threw away his greatest advantage, his superior numbers. He attacked in a series of smaller battles, securing local victories, but failing to destroy Lee's army. McClellan lacked the killer instinct that made Jackson so successful. He could not easily send his boys to their deaths. His ineffectual tactics at Antietam caused the war to drag on for over two more years and cost more lives than he would have sacrificed here."

A musket ball struck the latexsteel protection, and several tourists gasped. "It's time for us to leave."

Marden placed his hand on the window. "Those poor, brave boys," he said gravely.

Rafe was about to remove the latexsteel, when he looked back and surveyed the faces of his tour group. Someone was missing. Breathless, he said, *"Tarrant."*

Pushing through the group of tourists, Rafe saw the boy standing just within the four-meter range of the Ears' field, beside the tall, bearded man who had also carried a sketchpad.

Tarrant was holding out a handful of authentic gold pieces. "I've got lots of this stuff," Tarrant said. "If it's not enough, I can get more. Down the line, they hand it out like it's *candy*."

Surging forward, Rafe placed his hand on Tarrant's shoulder and drew the boy toward him. Tarrant tried to wriggle out of Rafe's grasp and uttered a string of twenty-first-century obscenities.

"Are you responsible for this boy?" The bearded man demanded. "He tried to bribe me to sketch one of the soldiers and put his face on it. Then he wanted me to create a portrait of his sweetheart, the blonde over there."

Kyla could not help but hear this. "His sweetheart?" she cried. "Not even in his dreams!"

If Tarrant could have shriveled and died at that moment, he would have done so gladly.

The man continued, "He doesn't seem to care that there's a war going on out there, or about the sacrifice those boys are making for him!"

Rafe did his best to steer Tarrant back to the group. "I am truly sorry, sir. It won't happen again."

Trying to regain some ground, Tarrant said, "Come on, Rafe. Don't you know who this is?"

Before Rafe could answer, Tarrant blurted out, "This is Alfred Waud, of *Harper's Weekly*. You know, the magazine *you* supposedly work for!"

"Yes, I heard what you said to Mr. Nicodemus,"

Waud said. "I was meaning to have a word with you when this was over about impersonating one of the press corps. I see I'll have to do it now."

Waud set his own sketchbook on the window ledge, snatched Rafe's sketchbook, and opened it. The first few pages of the book were filled with crude thumbnail sketches Rafe had made from photographs of the Antietam battle, with side notes describing each scene. Waud made murmurs of appreciation and surprise as he nodded and flipped through the pages. Then he stopped at a particular sketch, and the look in his eyes turned cold.

"What an interesting forgery," Waud said harshly.

Panic filled Rafe. He grabbed the book and shunted the group several weeks up the line.

Chapter Eight

"Completely uncalled for!" Dewey howled.

"Let's go over it one more time," Petric said mildly. "And let's keep our voices down."

Rafe sat between the two men on the train to Gettysburg. It had been impossible to book seats for all the tourists in a single car, so they were scattered throughout several carriages. The young Courier had lobbied for breaking into three groups, with Rafe looking after one, and Dewey and Petric supervising the other two. But the Patrolman and the probation officer had other ideas.

The prevailing attitude had been *We're on a train. We're in* motion. *How much trouble could the tourists possibly get into? Where could they possibly go?*

Rafe didn't even want to imagine the answers.

After shunting to a safe time after the battle, Rafe had retrieved the panels of latexsteel he had left on the windows of the little red farmhouse. Then he'd taken the group to a private house in Antietam that was renting out rooms. There they had spent the night.

In the morning, Rafe shunted the group three years up the line, and they traveled to the railroad station which at that time had not yet been closed.

The ride was bumpy, and the train rattled constantly. Rafe was being bounced around unmercifully on his seat.

And he was in the middle of an interrogation.

"I've already told you. There were sketches in my book from events that hadn't happened yet. I was hoping he would lose interest before he saw them."

"But he saw something that alarmed him," Petric said in his measured voice. "Are you saying that Alfred Waud now has information about the outcome of the war?"

"No. What he saw was a sketch I had made from one of his drawings. But the next page showed Lincoln's assassination. I couldn't let him see that. I grabbed the book and got us out of there."

"But once you had the book," Dewey said, "You didn't need to take such drastic action. We could have left when no one would have seen us go!"

Rafe shook his head. "We had already drawn too much attention to ourselves. What I did was acceptable damage control. Both of you know as well as I do that ever since the beginning of commercial time-travel, natives have been witnessing groups of tourists winking in and out of existence. If you stop to consider the number of tours that have already taken place—"

"Point taken," Petric said with a slight wave of his hand. "What about Tarrant? He's obviously a disruptive influence. I say we put him off the tour before he causes more trouble."

It took Rafe a moment to realize that he had been let off the hook—at least with the Patrolman.

"Tarrant," Rafe said softly. He had seen the way Tarrant was looking at Kyla. It was obvious that the boy was trying to get her attention. "I looked up the records on each of the tourists before we left," Rafe said. "Tarrant has been on several tours. His parents paid for all of them but never accompanied him. They're extremely wealthy."

"If his behavior here is any sign, they probably wanted to get him out of the way. The Time Service is not here to babysit spoiled brats."

"According to the retroactive damage clause of the standard tour contract, we could let him off with a warning and penalize their account," Dewey said. "That's a much better solution than the public-relations nightmare we could face by putting a child off a tour. Our branch will become a joke if word got out that we can't even keep children in line—"

The train suddenly lurched forward. Passengers were thrown backward and struck their heads on the hard wooden seats.

Rafe's first thought was to shunt up the line a few minutes, discover how the disturbance was about to occur, and stop it from happening. But if he shunted, he would materialize in midair, over the empty tracks where the train had not yet been or would soon approach. There was no doubt in his mind that one of the tourists was responsible for the sudden acceleration.

"Let's go," Petric snarled. "We've got to stop before the train shakes apart."

Passengers clogged the narrow aisle. Rafe, Petric, and Dewey forced their way through the crowd to the front of the carriage. Petric yanked the door open and looked out at the next car, just over a meter in front of him.

Petric leaped over the distance to the next car without hesitation. He tore the door open and flung himself inside.

Rafe and Dewey regarded each other. "I'll stay here and deal with the passengers," the instructor said.

The thought of one of his tourists alone and at the mercy of a Patrolman made Rafe leap across the narrow bridge. His right foot struck the platform, and his momentum carried him inside the opposite car, where he fell flat on his face. When he looked up, he could see Petric opening the door at the far end of the carriage. He tried to call out to the Patrolman, but the wind had been knocked from his lungs. He only managed a wheeze.

As Petric leaped to the next car, he looked like a man who was ready to pummel someone with righteous abandon.

Struggling to his feet, Rafe pushed through to the front of the carriage, then crossed to the next car. There he found Denise crouched in the aisle, trying to calm Jack and Margot Stuart, who were hysterical. Rafe's relief at seeing Denise was short lived. Tarrant was sitting a few rows down, reading a dime novel as if nothing were happening. The Stuart children, Kyla and Chuck, were nowhere in sight.

Denise looked up as Rafe hurried to her side. "They just vanished," she said.

"Did you see them go?"

"No, I wasn't even here. I came through after Petric. But the Stuarts claim that something exploded at the rear of the car, so everyone looked. When they turned around again, Kyla and Chuck were gone."

The breeze from the open windows assailed Rafe. He wondered if either Kyla or her brother knew enough about Time Belts to jury-rig their timers.

"Stay with them," Rafe said, then pushed his way to the empty seat behind Tarrant and sat down. Leaning forward, he shouted, "Tell me all about it, Tarrant, or you'll never come up the line again, so long as you live."

"They jumped," Tarrant said without turning.

For an instant, those two words gripped his heart, and he looked at the wide-open window and the rushing countryside beyond. Then the young Courier allowed himself to breathe.

"Nice try. Where did they go, Tarrant?"

The boy put his book down. "They went out the window."

Sticking his head out into the rushing air, Rafe saw a series of rungs to his left. Then he ducked back inside, closed his eyes, and shook his head.

"I've got them all this trip," he said incredulously.

"Have fun, sports hero," Tarrant muttered.

Taking a deep breath, Rafe leaned out the window, grabbed the closest rung with both hands, then leaped out of the train. There was a sharp, wrenching pain in his right shoulder as his body swung around and his boot connected with one of the lower rungs. Keeping his face turned away from the rushing wind, Rafe climbed up the rungs carefully. As he peered over the roof of the carriage, he saw a large, well-built, quivering mass lying on the rooftop, holding onto the train for dear life.

"Chuck! Where's your sister?"

Hands trembling, Chuck pointed ahead. Rafe turned but saw nothing at all. *Either she fell off the train or got where she wanted to go,* he thought.

"Chuck, I'm going to get them to stop the train! Can you hang on?"

There was a tight, high, affirmative squeal.

Rafe climbed back down. He found it considerably harder to get back inside the window than it had been to get out. Then he felt a hand grab his leg, and realizing someone inside was trying to help him, Rafe allowed himself to be guided back inside the train. Several hands pulled him through.

"Trying to get yourself killed or what, fool child!" a large man with fuzzy sideburns shouted. All but one of the people who had helped him were strangers. Denise backed away from the group and returned to the Stuarts.

"Chuck's on the roof!" Rafe shouted. He pulled away from the crowd and headed for the engine.

At last, crawling over an open carriage filled with coal, he reached his goal. Petric was already waiting. Kyla was covered with soot, and she was pouting. The conductor and his assistant were screaming at her. Petric was trying to get a word in.

"Devil's whelp!"

"Heathen!"

Petric turned to Rafe. "She threw her solar flare into the engine."

The girl shrugged. "It's just that we were moving so slowly. I gave the engine something more combustible."

"A solar flare?" Rafe said, not believing his ears. "So now what do we do?"

"Can't use brakes at this speed. We might jump the tracks. We'll just have to wait for it to burn out, make our apologies, and get off the train very, very quickly, before we're all lynched," said Petric.

Rafe told him about Chuck's current whereabouts. The Patrolman regarded Kyla, who tried to appear innocent.

No other words—except for the incessant stream of curses issued by the conductor and his assistant—were spoken until the flare burned out. At last they braked the train. The conductor's harangue continued even after the train was stopped.

Rafe gathered his tour group. He was relieved to find Chuck still clinging to the roof. After getting the young man down, they were put off the train at the next station.

Chapter Nine

As Rafe surveyed the train schedule given to him at the ticket office, it became clear that the tourists were in no mood for another bumpy train ride. Dewey was stooping in dark corners, recording complaint after complaint about the young Courier. A look of almost-psychotic impatience had appeared in Petric's usually good-natured face. He would have to take them down the line, finish the journey to Gettysburg in now-time, them shunt back the line to the time of the battle.

Rafe sighed and took them down the line. The station and the town surrounding it was now an all-but-forgotten ruin. A sign gave the exact times the hoverfloat would appear, and Rafe set their timers to the closest time and shunted. A huge silver vessel suddenly appeared; it was shaped like a cigar cut neatly in half and had a large flat deck covering its middle. A series of servant robots, or servo-bots for short, climbed from the hoverfloat. Rafe entered the float last and placed his thumb in the tiny window in the ferry-bot's open palm to pay for the trip. The mechanical's perpetual grin seemed to broaden a centimeter or two, then the ferry-bot welcomed Rafe aboard.

The quickest route was directly over the Potomac. During the ride, several tourists held on to the guard rail and peered over the side at the bright, shimmering waves; it was as if they had never seen a natural body of water.

Rafe noticed that Denise stood staring off at the horizon. She hugged herself, and one hand found its way to her face. Her little finger played absently with the corner of her mouth. The young Courier half expected either Dewey or the Patrolman to stop him before he got to her side; part of him even wished that would happen. But within seconds he was beside her.

For a time they didn't speak, though it was obvious she was aware of his presence. Feeling young, courageous, and stupid, Rafe decided to break the silence.

"How are you feeling?"

"What's that supposed to mean?"

"You just seem kind of tense. Something bothering you?"

She clutched her compression pack. "No."

"I missed you."

"Rafe, please don't." When Rafe didn't leave, she said, "I'm seeing someone else, okay?"

"Maybe we could still be friends," he said, cursing himself for a fool the instant the words were out. Not *friends*. Anything but that.

When she didn't respond immediately, his mind raced to find some way to undo the damage. Then, in a tiny voice all but lost in the wind, she said, "You mean that?"

"Yes," he said, and he meant it.

"Then be a friend," she said, "and don't ask any more questions."

With that she turned away.

Chapter Ten

GETTYSBURG, PENNSYLVANIA, JULY 2, 1863

The tourists stood on a tree-lined ridge, looking down into what had recently been a tranquil green valley. Soldiers overran it.

The hoverfloat was long gone. During the course of the trip, the female members of the group had spent time in the private chambers of the craft, applying their insta-seal facial appliances, phony beards, mustaches, and wigs. Then they changed into their much more comfortable male outfits. They were starting to get to tired. This would be the final event of the day.

Or so Rafe hoped.

"Major General Henry Heth of the Rebel army gained permission from his commander, A.P. Hill, to take his division on a quest for shoes, a precious commodity," Rafe said. "It was rumored that a cache of shoes could be found and liberated in the sleepy market-town of Gettysburg. The Rebels would chase away what they thought was 'the local militia,' then continue on. On July first—"

"Do I *have* to wear this stupid beard?" Kyla snarled. "This wig is way too tight!"

Jack Stuart cleared his throat, and both of his children fell silent. "You were saying?" he asked Rafe.

"Right. Yesterday, on July first, as the Rebels passed through Chambersburg Pike, they understood their mistake, and the battle began. The Union army was driven from Gettysburg, and most of the later fighting took place on the outskirts of town."

With careful planning and meticulous timing, Rafe led his tour group through many of the important conflicts during the first two days of the three-day battle. Some of the tourists complained at the amount of walking involved, but all agreed that it was worth the effort once they caught their first glimpse of the Federals' efforts to hold the high ground south of town. Despite the ferocious efforts of Lee's army, Culp's Hill and the Roundtops remained in the hands of the Federals, and the assault on Cemetery Ridge was turned away.

The tour group walked through the rocky hills and woods, and stood in the shadows of the cemetery gate-house. A thick fog surrounded them, the product of powder smoke from cannon and infantry rifles. Daylight was failing as the tourists watched the last battle of the second day. Afterwards, they went up the line to witness the earlier fighting. They visited the Pennsylvania College and the Lutheran

Seminary, which were used as observatories of the battle, and ended up back at Cemetary Ridge.

"A conflict north of the Potomac was inevitable from the moment Lee's plans became known. That it occurred here, on these three bloody days, was a surprise to both sides. On the second day, after forcing the Union lines back through the town of Gettysburg, the morale of Lee's forces was high. By the end of the day the mood had changed. Although he had suffered heavy losses, Lee was not about to admit defeat. He had enough strength left for one more offensive, and on July third, the final day of the battle, he mounted the attack that history recorded as Pickett's charge.

"There were three divisions in the assault, with a total of almost fifteen thousand Confederate men involved. But before the infantry was sent in, the great guns of the artillery sounded."

Touching the timer on his Master Belt, Rafe shunted the group down to the next morning and felt a rush of excitement as the massive lines of the Confederate artillery blinked into existence in the shallow, open valley west of Cemetery Ridge. There was no fighting, but tension hung heavily in the air. One hundred and forty Confederate cannons stood ready. Two guns were fired, one after the other.

"That's it?" Kyla whined. "When do we get to the good stuff?"

"That's the signal," Rafe said. "Now listen."

The loudest noise that any of the tourists could ever have imagined suddenly erupted: All of the

Confederate guns fired at once as Lee drove against the center of the Federal position on Cemetery Ridge. Soon the entire valley, two kilometers in length and half a kilometer in width, cradled a steaming maelstrom. Black smoke rose from the ground. The soldiers' guns fired in volleys, again and again.

Resetting his timer, Rafe took the group down to the final minutes of the artillery blasts. The smoke seemed to clear before their eyes.

"Two hours just passed," Rafe informed the group. "Next you're going to see the next stage of the Confederate advance from the side of the Federals."

Rafe shunted up the line to a safe time before the battle and ushered his group into the now-quiet valley. There was a slight incline, and they approached a low stone wall crowned with a wooden fence. They carefully climbed over the fence and walked to a small cluster of trees at the northern end of the cluster. Rafe activated his Ear, so that he would be alerted to any stragglers. Then he leaned against one of the trees and called for everyone's attention.

"See the little red eye in the knot of the hollow? That's a drone camera, one of several we've used to find safe pockets in the battle. For the next three minutes, not a single shot will come this way. Stay as close to this tree as you can. Our safe area is extremely limited. Is everyone ready?"

"Let's go!" Denise shouted, her voice plaintive. Rafe looked at her in surprise, then complied.

A filthy gray cloud enveloped the group. A chorus of gunfire and screams erupted. Shells exploded.

Tree limbs snapped and fell. The tourists saw figures bursting out of the mists, charging forward with their guns blazing. Sharp, deadly bayonets pierced the heavy smoke, probing the air before them. One gray-uniformed soldier paused to reload. Slamming the cartridge into the muzzle, he snapped the round home with his ramrod, shouldered the heavy weapon, and prepared to fire. He was cut down seconds later.

Union troops pushed through, and a brief skirmish took place four meters from the tourists. A tall, thin, straw-haired Union soldier in his late teens grappled with a barrel-chested, bearded Rebel for control of a single weapon that was pressed against their chests. They drew close. The smoky gray eyes of the young Federal soldier betrayed his fear and desperation.

At the edge of the safe area near the tree, Denise took a step forward, her gaze fixed on the struggle. She had torn off her facial appliances and dropped them to the ground, along with her hairnet and wig.

"No," she whispered.

Rafe turned suddenly. Denise was about to rush forward. He thrust his arm out to block her movement, then spun and grabbed her arms.

"You don't understand!" she screamed, clawing at him for freedom. The rest of her words were lost to rifle fire. Luckily Rafe's grip held fast.

In the middle of the conflict, the gray-eyed boy lost his footing and fell. The Rebel soldier lowered the gun to fire.

Denise screamed. For an instant the two men stood frozen. Then a bright red stain blossomed across the Rebel soldier's jacket. His expression was startled. The handsome blond Union soldier scrambled out of the way as the Rebel's body crashed to the ground. A ragged hole had been torn in the back of the man's gray jacket. He had been cut down from behind.

The blond soldier picked up his gun. His hair fell forward, into his eyes. His legs were unsteady. Suddenly he stiffened, as if he knew he were being watched. He spun, pointed his gun in the direction of the tourists, then froze as he saw Denise. Her little finger was hooked on the corner of her mouth.

As he lowered the weapon, his lips formed a single word: *Angel*.

Suddenly the young soldier's head snapped back as a bayonet tore through his chest. A dark-haired Rebel yanked the weapon back and ran forward as the blond boy fell face-forward.

The group of tourists watched as soldiers surged forward, stepping on the boy's body, driving it into the earth. Denise was screaming hysterically, fighting to break free.

Petric grabbed Denise from behind. "Shunt!" the Patrolman shouted.

Reaching toward his Master Belt's timer, Rafe saw that they had forty-five seconds left before the safe zone evaporated and the troops moved in. His fingers poised over the timer.

Then the bark of the tree beside his head exploded, sending a shower of wood and metal frag-

ments at his face. The red light of the drone camera
winked out.

The world became silent for Rafe, except for a
distant shrill tone that rose in volume and intensity
until it threatened to consume him. He stumbled
back from the tree, and dizziness and nausea threatened to overtake him. Someone brushed against him,
then thick smoke congealed around him, cutting him
off from the other tourists.

The Ear! he thought. The implant had been
damaged. He reached out and steadied himself on a
bristly tree-limb.

A figure broke from the haze. Denise was rushing in the direction of the fallen Union soldier, directly into the line of fire. She was almost enveloped
by the mist when a man surged forward and grabbed
her arms. A wall of smoke rose before Rafe, and
Denise was taken from his sight.

Shunt, he thought. *I have to shunt now!*

The world was spinning. He reached down to
his Master Belt and suddenly felt as if a weight had
fallen on his back, forcing him to the ground. His
hearing returned with a roar.

The smoke before him parted, and Denise
emerged. Tears streaked down her cheeks. When
she saw Rafe, a smile spread across her face. She
dropped to her knees beside him and took his
hand.

"The timer!" he cried out hoarsely. Despite the
roar of the battle and the high-pitched whine of the

malfunctioning Ear, she seemed to understand. Guiding his hand to the device, Denise rested her cheek against his. She closed her eyes as they shunted from the battle.

Chapter Eleven

"**W**hat a glorious display!" Jack Stuart shouted.

"Honey, it's quiet now, we don't have to scream," Margot reminded him.

Night had come, and the tourists had walked back to town. It was June twenty-ninth, the day before Heth's Rebel soldiers went on their expedition for shoes and the conflict began. Rafe didn't recall setting the timer for that date, but it was as safe a time as any to spend the night.

His injury was superficial. The fake beard and wig he had worn had taken the brunt of the damage from the flying splinters. The Ear had died completely, sparing Rafe the torture of listening to its incessant screams.

If only Dewey would follow its lead, Rafe thought.

"Unconscionable!" the instructor shouted. "Unpardonable! Unthinkable!"

Worse, Petric agreed with Dewey. The Patrolman even suggested taking the group back to now-
time, refunding their tickets, and charging Rafe with
reckless endangerment. The only problem was the
reaction of the tourists to their final moments in the
battle of Gettysburg.

They had loved every minute of it.

"Outstanding," Margot said.

"I'm impressed," Tarrant said grudgingly.

"I'm going to have my father write a feature
article on Rafe for the *Under D.C. Times*," Denise
promised.

"What's next?" they all demanded.

"Go on, Rafe," Petric said frostily. "Tell them."

"Tonight we'll get a good night's rest. In the
morning, we'll shunt down the line to Abraham Lincoln's famous delivery of the Gettysburg Address, in
November of 1883."

After they reached the hotel, Dewey cornered
Rafe and said, "This changes nothing. As far as I'm
concerned, you're finished. Enjoy this tour while
you can."

Chapter Twelve

Rafe couldn't sleep. He lay in the darkened room, feeling troubled and uncomfortable. From the instant the group had shunted out of the battle and up the line, he had had very little time to think about what had occurred. Now, in the solitude of his room, he had nothing *but* time.

The area he had chosen at Pickett's Charge was supposed to be safe, Rafe thought. The earlier findings of the drone camera had proven it. But the figures the drone had projected were standing still, remaining quiet. Denise's hysterics might have been enough to draw the attention of a soldier who would have fired first and examined his target later. It was a simple explanation, but something nagged at Rafe, something he couldn't quite identify.

The deafening sound of the tree being hit echoed in his mind. Suddenly he knew what had been bothering him: the sound was wrong. He had not heard a bullet striking metal and bark; the noise had come from the drone camera as it exploded. When he was a boy, Rafe's father had taken him to a firing range and taught him how to use several weapons, including a silent pulse rifle.

It was possible that someone else from now-time had been at the battle. If the drone camera had recorded his presence, he would have been forced to destroy it. They might not have been shooting at the tourists at all. What happened might not have been a result of Denise's actions.

He quickly surrendered to the overwhelming urge to go back to Pickett's Charge and examine the remains of the drone camera for evidence to substantiate his theory. In moments, he was dressed and had reset the timer of his Master Belt so that only he would be affected by it.

He would have to get Denise alone at some point and find out why she had been so upset by the fighting they had witnessed. She hadn't reacted that way at Antietam. If his new theory were wrong, her actions had placed the entire group in danger. He knew there must have been a reason for her to act so irresponsibly. Denise Chillington had a reason for everything she did, even for ending their relationship.

With a considerable amount of effort, he turned his thoughts from Denise.

He knew that the best way to leave unnoticed was to shunt to a time before the group arrived at the inn. That way he would not run the risk of attracting Dewey or Petric's attention. The only problem he could run into came from the popularity of the inn. It was likely that the room would be occupied, and he did not wish to be mistaken for a robber or worse when he suddenly appeared.

Simple enough. He would shunt from the hallway. If he surprised someone when he arrived, he would simply scowl at them and criticize them for sneaking up on him.

As he stepped into the hallway, he saw the glow of lantern light peaking out from beneath the door to Denise's room. He moved closer and realized that the door was ajar. Tapping on it gently, he whispered her name. Raising his voice slightly, he called to her. Nothing. He feared the door would squeak, but he pushed it open anyway.

The room was empty. Panic seized Rafe. He stepped inside, then quickly closed the door. He remembered the incident with Coffin trying to give General Jackson penicillin on his last tour. History was repeating itself.

He needed to think clearly, Rafe reminded himself. His options were limited. The least appealing course would be to wake Petric and tell him what had happened. But the tour would end right there, along with Rafe's career, and Denise would share the wrath of the Patrol. He couldn't allow that to happen.

No, he had to handle the situation himself. His timer was already reset. He had to find a hiding place, shunt up the line until Denise was present in the room, then wait until she was ready to leave and stop her. He glanced at her unmade bed. Apparently she had also tried to sleep and couldn't. Rafe reached

down and ran his hand over the slight indentation
left by her body. The mattress was cold.

His fingers unexpectedly grazed soft leather. A
small black book, easy to miss in the dim light, was
sitting open on the bed, its cover exposed. He picked
the book up, saving the place where Denise had left
off, and read the cover page.

It was the diary of Douglas Stanford Bannister.
The dates inside covered the years 1861 to 1863.
Denise had to have acquired it in now-time and
carried it up the line with her. Rafe began reading
selections at random.

Although Douglas had little formal education,
he was extremely intelligent. He had enlisted in the
Union army at the age of sixteen and had been
involved in a handful of conflicts.

Rafe's sense of patriotism was stirred by Douglas's vivid accounts of the battles. The day-to-day
struggles of the soldier's regiment were poignant
and startling. Rafe was not surprised when he read
the boy's confession that he hoped to one day become a great writer. The diary was a testament to his
incredible potential.

The final entries concerned the battle of Gettysburg. The last pages, scrawled in a different hand-
writing, told of a powerful encounter that had shaped
Douglas's final days. They had been written in a
nearby hospital after the boy had been fatally wounded
on the battlefield.

"I saw an angel standing in the corridors of Hell,
reaching out, calling my name in anguish, while demons held her back. . . ."

Rafe shuddered, then forced himself to read the final, shattering passages once again. He suddenly realized where Denise had gone and why. What she was doing was recorded history, and apparently it had always been such. To go back and stop her from leaving her room would have created a change in the past. But that didn't mean he had to let her go alone.

Positioning the book on the bed so that it appeared never to have been touched, Rafe hid in the clothes closet and peered between the slats. In thirty-minute shunts, he went up the line until Denise reappeared in the room. She sat on the edge of the bed, crying as she read the final entries in the diary.

Rafe felt a horrible pang of guilt as he watched her. But his discomfort at invading her privacy was pushed away by his need to protect her from the possible consequences of her own actions. The diary gave an idea of what she had done, but no indication of what had happened to her afterward.

Denise rose from the bed and wiped the tears from her face. Moving unsteadily, she opened the door, peered into the hallway, and left the room.

Rafe bolted followed her downstairs, past the sleeping man at the desk, and out of the inn. The streets were deserted. Her strides became more purposeful as she went on; her determination was evident. She walked the length of the town and headed toward a Union encampment on the outskirts of Gettysburg. The exact location had been given in the diary.

From a small copse of trees, Rafe observed as

Denise approached the young, straw-haired soldier on patrol. The young Courier recognized him instantly. In the woods at Pickett's Charge, Rafe had seen the boy run through by a rebel bayonet after he had been distracted by Denise. Today was June twenty-ninth. The Union soldier would be fatally wounded on July third, four days from now. But Denise had already experienced July third. By shunting back up the line to June twenty-ninth, she could warn him of his fate and attempt to save his life. Rafe wondered if that was what she planned to do, even though any interruption of the timestream was a serious timecrime.

A fine mist lay low over the ground. Denise looked as if she were floating across the surface of a cloud, as she closed the distance between herself and the soldier.

The moonlight bathed her white frilly dress in a luminous glow. She seemed more like an apparition than a beautiful young woman taking an evening stroll. When the soldier stopped her, she told him that she often took long walks late at night to combat her insomnia. They were near the valley where Harry Heth's Rebels would soon be engaged.

"I'm sorry, Miss. I must ask you to turn back to town."

She nodded gravely. "They said the war would never come this far north. That wretched Lee must be crazy if he thinks he can win a battle on this side of the Potomac. I'm surely glad you boys are here."

"Thank you, Miss," the soldier said. His gray eyes glinted in the moonlight like polished steel. "Miss?"

"Denise Chillington," she said and curtseyed.

From the woods where he hid, Rafe drew a sharp breath, even though he had read the soldier's diary and knew what would happen next. Denise suddenly rushed forward and kissed the startled soldier. At first he was taken back. A proper gentleman and lady from the Civil War era would never act in such a manner. Then the soldier must have seen the fear in her eyes and sensed that her actions were brought on by desperation.

"You *will* be safe," the soldier promised.

"I'm not worried about myself," Denise said softly. "I know you, Douglas Stanford Bannister. I know everything about you."

She told him of his life before the war, of the sister he lost when he was fourteen, and of the love he had always dreamed would come his way.

"What are you?" he gasped. "Are you an angel come to deliver me from the dangers of this war?"

"I could be."

"How could you know this?"

"I know that you would never turn away from your duty, even if it meant that you wouldn't live to see your family and friends ever again. It's a constant threat, and somehow you go on."

His lips pressed together in a thin white line. Muscles tightened in his face and neck.

"I've come a long way to tell you that your bravery will survive, that your courage and your need will one day touch more lives than you could ever dream, including mine."

"I don't understand."

"You don't have to. Just know that the love you've always sought is right here waiting for you." She placed her hand over his heart. "No matter what happens, I will always be here."

His hand covered hers. He drew it to his lips and kissed it gently. He was shaking.

"We must say goodnight," she said.

"Yes. Yes, of course," he said, releasing her hand and once again assuming his proper, gentlemanly stance. "A safe journey to you."

"And to you," she replied. Denise turned. She had taken three steps when Douglas whispered, "My angel."

She stopped and waited for Douglas to come to her side. Her little finger had found its way to the corner of her mouth. He took her in his arms without a word, embracing her as if she were the embodiment of life and love, a well of strength for him to draw upon. Their lips brushed lightly, then they shared a passionate kiss before he released her.

She seemed to be fighting the urge to cry once again as she walked away from him.

From his place of concealment, Rafe squeezed his eyes shut. He had the answers he needed. The pain that came with them would fade in time. Denise had not disrupted the timestream by telling Douglas that he would die in four days, despite her obvious desire to do so. Her presence in the camp that night was a part of history that she had played to perfection. He was proud of her.

Careful not to attract attention, Rafe headed back to Gettysburg. He followed Denise to her room at the inn. She stood at the doorway and without turning said, "Thank you."

Rafe was startled. He had been careful in following her. She couldn't have seen him. *Then how does she know I'm there?* he wondered.

She vanished inside her room, leaving the question unanswered. He considered following her inside, then decided against it. Walking from the inn once more, he traveled along the main section of street and soon left the confines of the town behind him.

He went to Cemetery Hill and found the small clump of trees where Douglas Stanford Bannister had fallen, mortally wounded. Then he located the tree where he had been standing during the battle, reset his timer, and shunted.

Suddenly it was the evening of July third, the night of the final day of the battle. Union troops were pulling out, preparing to go after Lee's men. Rafe examined the jagged crater in the wood of the tree where he and the tourists had been standing during the battle. The bullet had been dug out of the tree, along with the remains of the drone camera.

Someone had removed the evidence of another time traveler's involvement. Rafe thought about how to proceed. There was only one thing he could think to do: go back and grab the evidence before the gunman could get to it.

His heart was numb as he reset his timer for thirty seconds before his first appearance at Pickett's Charge. He was risking the Paradox of Duplication if his past-self became aware of his presence, so he would have to be very careful.

The information he had received from the drone camera had not revealed another safe zone during those fateful three minutes of Pickett's Charge. It did indicate, however, that no shots would strike the lower limbs of that same tree during that period. Gunners usually aimed high, so the bottom three meters of the tree would be safe.

Rafe climbed the tree, found a sturdy branch overhanging the spot where his group would appear, and shunted.

The calm of the quiet Pennsylvanian evening was shattered by the sudden intrusion of Pickett's Charge. His tour group materialized below him, and he watched the events he recalled from earlier in the day unfold.

In the small clearing, Douglas Stanford Bannister appeared, and Denise went berserk. Beyond the combatants, Rafe saw what looked like a shadowy figure watching the group from a vantage point several meters distant. It could have been a soldier, but the figure was standing very still, as separate from the action as Rafe was.

Suddenly the figure raised a weapon. Rafe saw three short, bright flashes, the unmistakable signature of a silent pulse rifle, and felt the tree quake under the impact. Below, the group scattered in panic. His past-self was nowhere to be seen.

Rafe leaped down from the tree limb, ready to grab the remains of the drone camera and shunt out of there, when a figure stumbled toward him and broke through the mists. It was his past-self, clutching his ear. Rafe had no time to move as his earlier incarnation bumped against him, then staggered away, swallowed up by the heavy smoke once more.

He didn't see me, Rafe thought, relieved. Above the din of battle, he heard Denise screaming, "Douglas!"

Turning in the direction of the shout, he saw Denise heading toward the fallen young soldier. She had broken away from Petric, and no one was moving to stop her.

Impossible, he thought. He remembered that when he was there the first time, he had seen a figure move from the tree and hold her back. He had assumed it was one of the tourists. But no one was moving to help her. In a second it would be too late. She would be out of the safe zone, wandering into a hail of bullets.

It was me, he realized in shock. *I saw my future self and didn't recognize him. Now I'm that future self, and it's up to me to save her!*

Just before she crossed over the line and vanished into the smoke, he rushed from the tree and took her by the arms. She froze at the sight of him.

"You can't save him," Rafe said.

"He's still alive!"

"Yes, and he's got to live long enough to dictate the final entry in his diary—the one you're going to see published when we go back to now-time."

Denise shook her head, her lips trembling. "You can't know that."

Rafe cursed under his breath. This version of Denise had not yet been to June twenty-ninth. It was only after this encounter that she would go back and leave her room to meet Douglas Stanford Bannister, inspiring him to write the words that would call from his time to hers and bring them together. Rafe knew there was only one way to convince her that he understood what she was going through.

" 'I saw an angel standing in the corridors of Hell, reaching out, calling my name in anguish, while demons held her back. She was my one true love. Four nights earlier she had called herself Denise Chillington. But to me she was my angel. With the memory of her kiss, I lay down my life without fear. I know that the Union will be saved, and that we will be together. Her kindness and mercy will live for eternity in these fragile pages, and in my heart.' "

The fight drained out of Denise. A single tear raced down her cheek. "You read it? The diary? How?" When he didn't answer, she said, "It's not you, is it? Your face is all right now. There are two of you here. You're from the future."

"Just a few hours later," Rafe said. "Long enough to know what's going on, finally. The one that's been hit, me from before, is over there." Rafe pointed.

She looked away. "I never meant to hurt you."

Gunfire sounded dangerously close.

"There's no time. This area's not safe. Anyway, we can talk after you see him."

Her eyes grew wide.

"Listen, this is important. The younger me, the one over there, his thoughts are scrambled. He's in shock. He can't set the timer. You have to help him do that. I'm going to give you the numbers to punch in. That will take you back four days. Douglas will still be alive and whole. Wait until after everyone's asleep, then go to him. I'll be following you to make sure you're safe."

Denise swallowed, trying to take it all in. "What about him? The other you. What do I tell him?"

"Nothing," Rafe said. "He doesn't know any of this yet, and he can't be allowed to find out until later. Put your light on and leave the diary on the bed when you go. That's how I remember it happening."

"I'll try," she said.

He gave her the numbers to memorize, then said, "We're traveling through time from different directions. What's already happened for me hasn't yet happened for you. As far as that Rafe Williamson is concerned, just the opposite is true. But we'll soon catch up to each other. Everything will be straightened out. Now go!"

She nodded and vanished into the smoke. He rushed back to the tree and found that the gunman had made it there before him. The remains of the drone camera were gone!

Suddenly a Rebel soldier broke from the dense fog before him and shouted in surprise at finding a civilian on the battlefield. It was too late for the soldier to turn his bayonet away from Rafe's chest.

Rafe hit the timer just as the sharp metal tore into his jacket.

Chapter Thirteen

It was night once more, and there was a slight tear in Rafe's jacket. By the time he made it back to the inn, slivers of orange and pink were stretching across the horizon. He was exhausted and in no mood to try to function without sleep. Also, he could not take the risk that his room might not remain undisturbed for the hours he had left it. Shunting to a few minutes before he had originally left his room, Rafe waited at the landing. When he heard his door open, he peered into the hallway and watched a nervous Rafe Williamson go out into the hall and see the light under Denise's door. Once his past-self was inside her room, he retired to his own room, flopped on the bed, and sank into a deep sleep.

Daylight was streaming into his bedroom when he awakened. It was June thirtieth. The Confederates and the Federals would be skirmishing soon. Rafe had just enough time to clean himself up, gather his charges for a quiet breakfast, then get them out before the soldiers arrived.

Twenty minutes later, he was sitting with Dewey and Petric in a private booth of the dining room. Two couples were having breakfast at the far end of the room, completely out of earshot.

"Sleep well?" Petric asked without indicating which of his companions he was questioning.

Rafe was wondering whether he should respond, when Denise arrived at the table and asked if she could join them. She sat beside Rafe.

"How do you feel?" she said softly. "Any hearing loss?"

"No, but my implant is shot."

A noise escaped Petric's lips: "*Hrummmm*." The Patrolman finished off his breakfast and continued to scrape his silverware against the plate as if he hadn't noticed that it was empty. "*Hrummmm*."

"Are *you* all right?" Rafe asked.

"Now," Denise said. "Now I am."

His hand was resting on his leg. She put her hand over his and gave it a strong squeeze.

"I'm glad you're here," he said.

"Me too."

Petric looked up sharply. He sniffed the air. Then he allowed his gaze to settle on his empty plate, which he regarded with confusion.

Rafe barely noticed the Patrolman's behavior, although Denise became quite uncomfortable when Petric's gaze fixed on her.

"Good morning, Mr. Petric."

He let out that noise again, "*Hrummmm*," this

ime accompanied by a frown. "You work in the
museum Jack Stuart runs," Petric said. "Went to school
with his children. Had an *affair* with Rafe. Marden's
one of the museum's patrons and supporters. Tarrant's
parents contribute funds. You all know one another."

Dewey followed the Patrolman's lead. "I hadn't
thought of that," he said.

"I'm not surprised," Petric said.

"Your attention, please."

Rafe looked up and saw a red-uniformed porter
standing before their table. He held a package perhaps a meter square and only a few centimeters
thick. It was neatly tied with a string.

"I have a delivery for Mr. Rafe Williamson," the
porter said.

"There must be some mistake," Rafe said.

"No mistake, sir." Rafe gave the man a generous
tip in local currency. The porter handed the package
to Rafe with a forced smile.

Rafe scanned the wrapping on the package.
"There's no address. Where did this come from?"

"It must have been delivered during the night,"
the porter said. "Our night man said that he simply
turned around and saw it sitting behind him."

"I see," Rafe said.

"Will that be all, sir?"

"For now," Rafe said. "Thank you."

Disappointment flashed over the porter's face.
He turned and walked off.

"Aren't you going to open it?" Denise said.

Setting the package on the table, Rafe untied the
string and was about to poke a hole in the paper

with his fork when Denise rose suddenly and grabbed his arm. "Be careful!"

Her outburst surprised the young Courier.

"I'll do it," she said. Nudging Rafe to one side, she made a tiny incision on the side of the package, then went to work on tearing the paper apart. When she was finished, they were looking at an unframed painting.

The knowing smile immediately drew their attention. So did the familiar state of repose, the gently folded hands.

" 'Arrangement in Grey and Black,' " Denise whispered in awe and surprise. "James Whistler's most famous work."

Even Dewey recognized the portrait, although he knew it by the name most of the world had come to accept.

" '*Whistler's Mother*,' " he said. "This is a masterpiece. Priceless. What's it doing here?"

"Listen to me. You don't understand," Denise pleaded. "Mrs. Anna McNeil Whistler isn't even going to board the blockade runner from the Cape Fear River in North Carolina until the end of the year when she goes to visit her son in England. It's during that visit that he paints her portrait. We're holding something that doesn't even exist yet!"

Chapter Fourteen

Taking the wrapping paper in his hand, Petric brought it to his face and sniffed. "Charanea XII. That's what I've been smelling!"

Rafe looked to the Patrolman in confusion.

"It's a perfume from now-time. My wife always wants me to buy it for her, but it's too expensive. Someone smuggled this back from our time. The question is—why?"

"I'll tell you why," Dewey said excitedly. He rose up and pointed at Rafe. "*He's* a thief!"

"That's ridiculous," Denise said.

"No," Rafe said, already trying to fit the pieces of the puzzle together. "It makes sense. The black-market value for an item like this could set a Courier up for life. The only problem is, I'm innocent."

Petric shook his head. "I want to see something. Show me your timer."

Rafe felt his breath catch in his throat. A moan

of defeat welled up inside him, but he held it in check as he complied with the Patrolman's wishes.

"Just as I thought. Your timer's set to manual Courier control. Where were you last night, Rafe?"

The Courier was silent.

"I can answer that," Denise said. She relayed the events of the previous evening. "I knew he was following me. I could sense him the whole time."

"Did he return to the inn with you?"

Before Rafe could answer, she said, "Yes. We spent the whole night in my room. *Talking*."

The Patrolman frowned and looked back to Rafe. "You must have made the arrangements to have your stolen goods delivered here before you knew Dewey and I would be on this little tour. Then you had no way of canceling the order."

"Oh, right. So why didn't I get the painting and stash it in my compression pack while the rest of you were asleep? Letting it sit there would make me a pretty stupid criminal."

"Or the Patrol is closing in on your accomplices in now-time," said Petric. "The criminals needed a place to hide the evidence. They knew your schedule and delivered the painting here."

"We're on an unscheduled stop," Rafe protested.

The Patrolman shrugged. "They viewed the records after this tour and learned where you would be. Or they spoke to one of the returning tourists. All I want you to do is answer one simple question, Rafe. Who are your accomplices?"

"I'm innocent."

Petric shook his head; his mind was obviously

made up. "Why don't you just confess and make my job a little easier?"

Denise broke in with, "What job?"

"He's a Patrolman," Rafe said. "Can't you tell?"

Petric flinched. "Look, Courier, the only reason I'm not taking you back right now is that I want the people you're working with."

Rafe was about to protest when the Patrolman clamped his hand on the back of Rafe's neck. "If I settle for you, your friends will go so far underground we'll never find them. If we keep going, they might trip up again. And this time I'll be waiting. Now, take off your Master Belt and give it to Dewey. If you try to escape, I'll drive your windpipe into the edge of this table. Understood?"

"Yes," Rafe said solemnly. He complied with Petric's orders. The Patrolman released his grip.

"Dewey, give him yours."

"Do you really think that's wise?" Dewey asked anxiously. "I think we should end the tour now."

"Just do it," Petric ordered.

The instructor removed his Time Belt and handed it to Rafe.

"I want to go on," Rafe said. "I want to finish the tour. I want time to clear my name."

"I hope you can," the Patrolman said.

Rafe was startled. "You admit that I might be innocent?"

"Of course," Petric said. "Working for the Service, I've come to regard *anything* as possible."

Rafe and the others agreed not to mention the disturbing events that had begun their morning.

Petric removed his own compression pack and confiscated the painting as evidence. After restoring the pack to its billfold size, he stuffed it in the pocket of his jacket.

Margot Stuart appeared, without her husband. She smiled at Petric, and the two of them retired to another table, leaving Dewey to watch the young Courier. Denise stared at one of the paintings hanging on the wall midway through the dining room.

"I don't know why I didn't notice that before," she said. She rose from the table and walked toward the painting. Rafe and Dewey followed. "We have this one in our museum. It's William Sidney Mount's 'Dancing on the Barnfloor,' from the eighteen fifties."

There were several paintings in the lobby. Denise gravitated toward the first one and shuddered. After examining two more paintings, she turned to Rafe and said, "These weren't here last night. They shouldn't be here at all. This one was created in 1871. The other two are from the early 1880's."

"Incredible," said Rafe.

"No," Denise said. "The incredible part is that right now every one of them, including 'Arrangement in Grey and Black,' is supposed to be hanging in the Under D.C. Museum!"

Chapter Fifteen

The tourists purchased winter clothing then shunted down the line to the brisk November morning of the famous Gettysburg Address, in 1883. Enormous crowds lined the streets as a military parade passed through the center of town. Fifteen thousand people had gathered here for the day. The people cheered as President Lincoln rode through on horseback, smiling cheerfully despite the opening symptoms of a case of smallpox.

The crowd cheered as Lincoln stood, a single sheet of paper in his hand. In just under three minutes, in his thin, high-pitched voice, Lincoln delivered the ten lines that would withstand the test of history.

The reaction of the crowd was somewhat less enthusiastic.

"That's it?"

The tall man with a gray beard standing beside Marden repeated his question.

A spattering of dutiful applause came from the crowd as the President sat down once more.

"Marden?"

The historian turned. Tears streamed down his face.

"What a glorious journey this is," Marden said.

Rafe gathered the tourists and explained that the true greatness of the Gettysburg Address was not realized until much later. The polite but cold reaction of the audience and of the visiting dignitaries was mirrored by the press, who either overlooked the speech or openly criticized Lincoln's words.

"I thought he was supposed to have this low, deep voice," Chuck said, mimicking the baritone delivery he had expected from the President. "He does in all the holo-vids."

Rafe gave his standard speech about the way Old Hollywood often distorted facts for dramatic effect, and about how the practice was still going on in now-time.

"If there are no more questions, Dewey will take us out of here."

Kyla ground her hands into her hips. "I have a question. Why is *he* shunting us instead of you?"

"Rafe's timer was damaged in the battle, when he tripped," Denise said. "Dewey has a Master Timer, too, and insisted on doing the honors."

The instructor glared at her. His pudgy face turned pink, despite the chill in the air. "Yes," he said slowly. "That must be it."

Denise linked her arm with Rafe's, and they went down the line.

Chapter Sixteen

They shunted to Christmas of 1890 and took the evening train from Gettysburg to Washington.

Rafe had chosen the year 1890 because at that time many of the cars were more comfortable and spacious than during the Civil War. The dinner menu offered twelve courses and forty-five dishes.

The dining cars featured comfortable, beautifully upholstered seats, inlaid woods of various colors, ornate lighting fixtures, plate-glass mirrors, velvet drapes, and plush carpeting. Denise joined Rafe for their meal. Petric sat at a table with Margot. Margot's husband, well over the shock he had received back at the inn, had struck up a conversation with Dewey and Marden. Kyla and her brother dined with Tarrant. Kyla was making a show of warming to poor Tarrant, as if to inflame Rafe's jealousy. Rafe was delighted she was leaving him alone, but he worried about the effect she was having on Tarrant. The boy was hopelessly lovestruck. When his attentions no longer amused her, Kyla would drop him without a second thought, and he would be devastated.

"There's nothing you can do," Denise said. "Your job description only covers so much."

"I still feel responsible."

"Rafe, she's only interested in you for two reasons. First of all, you don't want her, and that makes her crazy."

The young Courier leaned forward. "What's the other reason?"

Denise looked down at her meal. "This is too fast," she said.

"I know. I'm sorry."

She squeezed his arm. "No, don't be. We're good together," she said.

Changing the subject, Rafe said, "I'm *dying* here. Someone's gone through a lot of trouble to set me up, someone who really wants to bury me. Thing is, I have no idea who would want to do this. None."

"All right," she said. "You were there for me. I'm going to be there for you."

"I don't need sympathy, I need...."

"I know." She closed her eyes and let out a heavy breath. "Tell me everything, one more time."

Rafe went through his entire story, ending with his bizarre discovery at Pickett's Charge.

"So someone didn't want his picture taken," she said.

"Uh-huh," Rafe said. Then he smiled. "Can we stop calling this person *someone*?"

She sighed. "What do you want to call him?"

Rafe licked his lips. "We'll call him *The Razor*. This person's sharp and deadly."

"You're an idiot," she giggled. "You haven't changed a bit."

He returned her smile. "You don't like it?"

"*The Razor?* Rafe, where do you come up with this stuff?"

"That's what I'd like to know," a thick, harsh voice said.

Rafe and Denise looked up to see a young, dark-haired steward standing beside their table. He held a covered serving dish. His eyes were perfectly black, his forehead sloped, his eyebrows shaved away. His nose had been broken. Long sideburns seemed to point inward, to his thin lips and scarred chin. Thin white gloves covered his hands.

Without pausing, the steward removed the cover from his dish, revealing a long straight-razor. The man grabbed the weapon and lunged at Rafe.

Denise screamed and threw herself across the table, grabbing the man's arm as it arced downward. Rafe slid down in a lightning-quick motion. His back against the seat, his head pressing against the wall of the carriage, he kicked the man in the gut with all his strength. The man stumbled backward, dragging Denise into the aisle.

The carriage was suddenly alive with screams and confusion. People rose from their seats, straining to see. At the far end of the carriage, Petric rose from his table and leaped on top of it. He bounded from table to table without a sound, a look of intense determination on his face.

Rafe's assailant had not lost his grip on the razor. He swung it downward toward the seat where the young Courier had been only seconds before, and slashed open the rich upholstery.

Rafe leaped at the man just as Petric launched himself from the opposite table. The three men crashed together. Denise fell back from the mad tangle of screaming Courier, Patrolman, and would-be killer. They struck the aisle with a thud.

When Rafe and Petric climbed to their feet, the third man was gone.

Chapter Seventeen

"**I** *knew* you were lying," Petric said.

He and Rafe were in the smoking car; their cuts and bruises were being nursed by Denise and Margot.

"It looks like your friends in now-time want to get to you before you talk," Petric said. "Why are you still covering for them?"

Rafe knew it was pointless to argue, so he shut up.

Slapping his hands on his knees, the Patrolman rose. "I believe I can leave you two alone for a few minutes. Whoever your friend was, shunting from a moving train had to have been a big mistake. I'm sure he's in no condition to come after you for awhile. And if he has partners, they'll have to wait until we stop before they can get on."

The Patrolman went off to the lavatory at the end of the carriage and vanished inside. Rafe leaned close to Denise and commented "Something Petric said before really disturbs me."

"Everything Petric says disturbs me," Denise countered.

"Whoever's doing this has to know *exactly* where we're going to be at any given moment of this tour, including the unscheduled stops. The only people who could know that are *on* this tour. It's possible that someone here is making notes of everything that's happening and at exactly what time it occurs, so they can use it later."

"Or that might have been what our friend was doing at Pickett's Charge."

"And before. But there's something else."

"You think it's one of us," she said, remaining fixed on that point. "One of the tourists."

"It's possible, yes. You see—"

"Even me," she added. "I'm suspect."

There was an uncomfortable pause before Rafe answered. He grinned and said, "Not unless you use Charanea XII."

"You really are an idiot," she said.

"No, I don't think it's you. But if someone's setting me up, they might be setting you up, too."

She considered this and twisted back and forth in her seat. "Because we know each other."

"And because you know what pieces are valuable and you have access to the Under D.C. Museum. You said that all those paintings at the inn are also on display there. Mr. Stuart runs the museum. His wife and kids have access at any time. Tarrant's parents and Marden are supporters and have connections that way. They all get special privileges. Everyone's a suspect."

The realization hit her hard. "Tell me the rest."

"Denise," he said, "I'm not sure what to do."

"You'll think of something," she said. "You will."

She looked up and saw Petric making his way back.

"Did I miss anything?" the Patrolman asked.

The noise of the train filled the gap left by their silence.

"I've made a decision," Petric said. "You're obviously not fit to control this tour. And I believe the attempts on your life will continue. I don't want the tourists placed in danger."

"You're canceling the tour?"

"Not at all," Petric said. "I'm putting Dewey in charge."

Chapter Eighteen

The evening train arrived in Washington on schedule. A crowd waited at the station, eager to embrace loved ones just arriving.

"Ladies and gentlemen, welcome to the capital," Dewey said, but the tourists were busy pushing through the crowd. Dewey allowed Rafe to lead his charges out to the street, where they fought bitterly for a horse carriage.

Finally, baggage secured and everyone in place, Rafe barked, "The Willard Hotel!"

A moment later they were off. The streets were clogged with traffic, and it seemed as if hours had passed before they reached the hotel. After checking in, Denise and Jack Stuart examined a few of the paintings in the massive lobby. By the time they were done, Stuart was frantic.

"More anachronisms," Denise explained to Rafe. "All from the museum."

"Maybe we shouldn't stay here," Dewey said. "It might not be safe. Rafe's accomplices know where we are."

"All the better," Petric said. "Maybe this time we can snare one of them."

The White House was within walking distance.

"It's always been a dream of mine to meet the President," Marden said, his voice quavering. "Now it's really going to happen!"

Rafe was walking beside him. "Remember, there are no guarantees he'll be receiving."

"I understand," Marden said excitedly.

Dewey cleared his throat.

"I suppose this is a good time to tell you all that Mr. Carollan will be your Courier for the duration of this tour," Rafe said. "I trust you will show him every respect you've shown me."

"This ought to be good," Tarrant muttered, a nasty edge in his voice.

Rafe wondered if Kyla had finally given Tarrant his walking papers. The two seemed to be ignoring each other.

When they arrived at the White House, Rafe displayed his press pass, and they were taken through the gates, past the blue-uniformed soldiers of the Bucktail Brigade (so named for the strips of fur in their caps), and into a large, modestly furnished room. Only three people were in line, before them. A quarter of an hour passed, and two of the three people ahead were ushered inside.

Petric approached and leaned in close. "If you're

going to be the Courier, you had better start acting like one."

Swallowing, Dewey rose and said, "While we wait, a few important historical details."

The tourists gave the instructor their attention. Dewey looked around, in confusion. Rafe realized the instructor didn't *know* any important historical details. "This room, it is, um, quite historically significant, naturally, for its size and modest furnishings."

The tourists stared at him. Dewey shifted uneasily, then went on. "And this, of course, is a chair. A solidly designed chair. Good and sturdy. Most definitely, certainly, a chair."

Getting colder. Rafe sat and found something to read.

"Rafe," Dewey said solemnly, "Is there anything you wish to add?"

Rafe said, "Lincoln wants to end the war. A week ago today he conducted peace meetings at Hampton Roads, Virginia, without success. Five days ago he presented a plan to the Cabinet that would have the Federal government pay four hundred million dollars to the slave states if they would put down their weapons by the first of April. The Cabinet unanimously opposed the plan, and it was dropped.

"Also, the fight is on for the ratification of the Thirteenth Amendment. The House of Representatives has passed the Constitutional amendment, which would abolish slavery. But three fourths of the states must pass it as well. Maine and Kansas just ratified the amendment, Delaware did not. Unknown to all, the end is near, for both the war and the great man himself."

The door to Lincoln's office opened, and the stocky man in the dark uniform beckoned. "Oh," he said. "You people are back."

Dewey adjusted his jacket once more and led the tourists inside Lincoln's office.

Chapter Nineteen

The sight of the President standing before him was almost enough to make Dewey lose his newfound adventurous spirit.

"Mr. President," Dewey said as Lincoln came from around his desk and shook the instructor's hand. "D.W. Carollan. I would like to present a group of people who have traveled a long way to meet you."

One by one, the tourists were introduced to the President. Lincoln's grip was incredibly strong.

Marden was trembling as the President extended his hand. "The Ford's Theater," Marden stammered. "John Wilkes Booth has said that he intends to shoot you with his single-shot Derringer on the fourteenth of April, at the evening performance of 'Our American Cousin.' He must be stopped!"

The stocky man in the dark uniform was moving toward the historian. Lincoln raised his hand, and the man stopped. Rafe and Petric, also about to lay hands on Marden, froze. As inconspicuously as possible, Petric twisted his wrist three times, allowing his palm holo to fall into his hand. It began recording.

"These are serious allegations, my good fellow;" the President said. "This actor, Booth you said? You heard him make such threats?"

Marden nodded.

"Don't worry. It's nonsense. Why would anyone want to assassinate me? If they were moved to do so, they could do it whenever they pleased, as long as they are ready to exchange their life for mine."

The right hand of the stocky gentleman in black was inside his jacket pocket.

"He will," Marden pleaded.

"I see," Lincoln said. He stepped back, lowering his hand. "You have done your duty well. One of my aides may have a few questions before you leave."

Rafe was stunned. The stocky man herded the tourists toward the door as Lincoln walked back to his desk. Dewey was shaking as they returned to the waiting room.

Rafe came up beside him and whispered, "We have to get out of here. Set the timer for early this morning."

"But we'll still be in the White House!" Dewey said. "Rafe, you'll have to do it!"

"I can't," Rafe said, "You're wearing my timer."

The instructor reached beneath his jacket and touched the timer.

Time didn't seem to pass at all, but they were surprised to find the stocky man walking toward them, when just seconds ago, he had been behind them. He didn't seem to recognize them.

"May I help you?"

"The President," Dewey said in a strained voice. "We were here to see the President."

"I'm sorry, it's a bit early for that. Come back this afternoon. He may have some time for you then. For now I'll have to escort you out."

"Thank you," Rafe said. They were outside the gates of the White House moments later. Marden fell to his knees, hyperventilating.

"What have I done?" the historian cried.

"That's a good question," Petric said. He looked to Dewey and said, "We're going to have to fix this. Someone peel Marden off the ground. We're drawing too much attention. Dewey, we need to—"

"Not me!" Dewey screamed. "I can't. I'm sorry, I can't." He ripped the Master Belt from his waist and held it out to the Patrolman. "You do it. Let Rafe do it. I don't care. Just not me!"

The Patrolman stared at the instructor with contempt and took the Master Belt from Dewey's trembling hand. Without taking his gaze from the older man, Petric said, "Rafe? Are you up to this?"

"Yes."

"Then let's go somewhere more private."

They walked back to the Willard Hotel, Jack Stuart and Petric supporting Marden. The historian's will seemed to have left him; he was crushed by what he had done.

They arrived at the hotel.

Dewey was in slightly better shape, and he was

left in charge of the remaining tourists, who waited in the massive lobby of the hotel.

"Aren't you going to leave me a timer?" Dewey asked, his eyes wide with fear. "I don't want to be trapped in another era!"

Petric didn't bother to answer. Rafe took Jack's place and helped Petric escort Marden upstairs. Once they reached Marden's room, Rafe and Petric dumped him on the bed.

"How do you want to work this?" Rafe asked.

Petric removed the Master Belt from his jacket and keyed in a series of numbers. "I'm punching in the temporal I.D. code of my timer. Our Time Belts will be the only ones affected by this shunt."

Suddenly the room was occupied by an elderly couple in their nightrobes. They both shouted in fear and surprise as the time travelers appeared.

"Hotel security, routine check," Petric said. He hurried out of the room, Rafe directly behind him.

"So, when are we?" Rafe asked.

"Saturday, April fifteenth," Petric said. "Easter weekend. The day after Lincoln's assassination. Let's find a newspaper."

A small boy had set up a stand in one corner of the lobby. They rifled through every newspaper he sold. Finally Rafe found a small article about Lincoln attending a special performance at Ford's Theater the previous night.

"Lincoln's alive. The President's security men must have dealt with Booth."

Outside the hotel, Rafe and Petric maintained a casual pace until they were several blocks from the hotel. The White House loomed at the far end of Pennsylvania Avenue. The Patrolman turned to Rafe and said, "I know what's happened, but we need documentation. Any ideas?"

"That depends on what you have in mind for Marden when we get back," Rafe said. "He doesn't deserve prosecution."

Petric stopped cold. His index finger suddenly appeared and began poking at the young Courier's chest. "Are you trying to make demands on *me*? Marden committed a serious timecrime. Do I need to remind *you* that it was a situation very much like this one that got you into trouble in the first place?"

"I want you to issue a pardon for Marden. Do that and I'll cooperate in every way."

"Including naming your accomplices?"

"I keep telling you," Rafe began, then realized his protests were futile. An idea began to form in his mind, and he said, "You want to continue this investigation because you're not a hundred percent sure I'm guilty. You think there might be other suspects in the group, and that if they learn you're a Patrolman, you'll never get anything from them. Tell me the truth or I'll ruin your cover. And then, when we're back in now-time. I'll name you as one of my accomplices!"

A long, throaty sigh came from the Patrolman. He clicked off the palm holo and slipped the device in his pocket. "Yes. I'm investigating the forgeries."

"They're not authentic?" Rafe said in surprise.

"Whoever's behind this has been making a fortune duplicating precious works of art for private collectors throughout time. They've been going into the past and smuggling out the identical materials the artists used to create the originals. The exact same canvases, pigments, brushes—everything. They steal the original and bring it down the line to now-time for their forgers to study, sometimes for weeks, we guess. Then they go back up the line and return the originals, maybe only seconds after they took them in the first place. After that they store the forgeries in a vault somewhere so that they age the proper number of years and under the correct climate.

"As far as we can tell, this has been going on for years. At times, they've even stolen from one client to satisfy the needs of another, provided they were from different eras. The problem is, the criminal has gotten sloppy. The original and three duplicates of a certain painting came into the public eye at the same time in history, when no records of forgeries existed. It happened in France. A duel was fought over the authenticity of one of the portraits, and a man who was supposed to father a line of generals was killed, affecting history. That was easy enough to solve. But now that we know the operation exists, whoever's behind it doesn't want to be caught. If you're telling the truth, Rafe, that's why you were set up."

Rafe was stunned. "But why did you decide to investigate *my* tour?"

"We searched the homes of every active Courier while he or she was away up the line. One of the paintings was found in your apartment."

Rafe looked at the Patrolman and said, "You

didn't have to tell me any of this. Why did you?"

"Because I'd already ruled out Marden as a suspect. But you wanted to defend him anyway. My instincts tell me that someone with that kind of decency couldn't be behind the forgeries."

"Decency? I'm talking about obstructing justice, according to the Service."

"Rafe, you're not the only one who bends the rules sometimes. We all do it. You were just unlucky enough to get caught. But there is one other problem. My instincts aren't always right. That's why you're not off the hook."

"All right," Rafe said. "Do we have a deal about Marden?"

"Yes," Petric said. "So where do you think we should go? We're going to need something to show Marden."

"Only one place we can go," Rafe said.

"Where's that?"

"Where else?" Rafe said. "The future."

Twenty minutes later, they were dropped in front of the Ford theater. "We should go about eight months down the line," Rafe suggested.

They shunted, and suddenly it was freezing cold. There was snow on the ground, and it was late in the evening.

"Perfect," Rafe said. "There's a bar near the theater where all the actors go after their performances. I'm sure we can find someone to help us there."

Soon they were in Taltavul's saloon, just east of the Ford Theater. They spent about an hour throw-

ing around money and inquiries, then were joined
by a seedy-looking old man who smelled of lilac. His
nose was crooked, as if it had been broken many
times, and a single gray eyebrow stretched across his
forehead, hanging above his dark, almost black eyes.
Deep lines and scars covered his face where his
scraggly white beard did not grow. His gnarled fingers poked from holes in his black gloves. Oddly
enough, his teeth were perfectly white.

It took both Rafe and Petric several minutes to
realize they were in the presence of a very young
actor who hadn't bothered to change out of costume.

"Booth?" the actor cried. "They've got him locked
up with all the other die-hard Reb lovers, the ones it
just ain't safe to have on the streets! Yes sir, they got
Booth and Mary Surratt and that other feller, ah,
Lewis Payne, that's it! Can you imagine? Those fools
conspiring to kill the President?"

Petric's palm holo dutifully recorded every word.
A few minutes later, after paying off the actor, they
emerged from the bar. Rafe turned to Petric and
said, "It's not hard to imagine why Marden did it.
There's a part of me that wants to leave this alone.
Lincoln deserved to see peace come to the states, to
see the divided Union come together once again."

"I see," Petric said suspiciously.

"I just mean that I understand, not that I would
do it myself."

Petric took a moment, then said, "You want to
see him, don't you? Lincoln, alive."

"No, absolutely not," Rafe said. "That'll make it

too hard to do what we have to do. I'd feel like an assassin myself."

"Now you're starting to understand what a Patrolman goes through. You Couriers think our tough shells come from indifference. Sometimes that's true. Not always."

Rafe was startled. "Thomas, I—"

Shaking his head, Petric whispered, "We have some editing to do. Come on."

They arrived at the Willard Hotel and shunted to twenty minutes before the tourists' arrival. The room that would be Marden's was at the far end of the third-floor corridor. After waiting for the hallway to clear, Petric removed a small kit from his pocket and picked the lock. They were inside the room in seconds.

"Are you sure about this?" Rafe asked as he positioned himself behind the door.

"Of course," Petric said. "So long as our earlier selves don't see us, we're fine. The Paradox of Duplication is the last thing I want to deal with."

"But we're about to wipe out the chain of events that led us to leave the group in the first place," Rafe said. "Won't that *cause* the Paradox of Duplication?"

"Only if we're careless," Petric said.

The door opened, and Marden entered. The historian seemed giddy. Then he shrieked as he saw Rafe and Petric.

"Sit down, William," Rafe said as Petric removed his palm holo.

The gaunt man seemed terrified.

"There's something we have to show you."

Chapter Twenty

After viewing the holes, Marden confessed that saving the President had always been his greatest fantasy. In fact, he had been thinking about it when he entered his room and found Rafe and Petric waiting. But he never thought he would actually go through with it.

"I'm so sorry," he said gravely. "I know what you must do. Take me back to now-time."

"That won't be necessary," Petric said. He reached behind his back and removed a pair of authentic handcuffs from the rear of his vest. Rafe caught a glimpse of other shiny metallic objects hidden beneath the Patrolman's jacket as Petric handcuffed Marden to the bed.

"I'm sorry, William." Rafe looked away from the historian. "We can't allow you anywhere near Lincoln right now."

Marden lowered his head and held back his tears until Rafe and Petric had left the room.

They were in the hallway when Rafe said, "Meeting Lincoln was his dream."

"Don't feel sorry for him," Petric said. "He got off easy, just like we agreed."

In the lobby, the remaining tourists were gathered with Dewey. The women paraded before a full-length mirror, amazed at how wonderful the clothes made them look, despite how restrictive the dresses were.

"What happened?" Dewey demanded. "The two of you vanished, along with my Master Belt! Rafe was right in the middle of a sentence, then both of you were gone!"

Rafe understood. It was exactly as Petric had explained it earlier: They had relegated their past-selves, the duplicates, to a parallel timeline that had been edited from existence.

Petric yanked Dewey aside and relieved him of command. Dewey whined, until Petric finally played back the holos, which made everything clear to the pudgy man.

Petric went to Rafe and explained the new rules. "Do your job well, Courier. I'll handle the Master Belt. You take care of the tourists."

"I'll do that," Rafe said. He turned to address the tourists. "People, I'm afraid that William won't be joining us for the next leg of our tour. All the excitement has tired him out. But the rest of you are about to meet one of the truly great figures in history. I'll fill you in as we walk over to the White House."

Just as they left the hotel, a scruffy old man smelling of lilacs bumped into Rafe. He grinned at the young Courier with a set of perfectly white teeth. It took Rafe a moment to recognize the young actor from the bar. Rafe thought it was odd that the man was wearing the exact same costume he had worn eight months in the future.

"I hope what I told you was helpful," the actor said.

"Yes, very," Rafe said. Then he froze in shock. This version of the actor was eight months younger than the one they met down the line—in an alternate time-line that had just been wiped from existence. There was no possible way for him to remember their conversation.

Rafe felt the cold muzzle of a gun press against his stomach. He looked down to see that the actor carried a single shot Remington.

"Bang, bang," the actor said, and vanished before Petric could lay a hand on him.

"It was him," Rafe said, his heart thundering. "The man from the train. I should have recognized him right away."

"How could you with that makeup job?"

"That's the point. Makeup in this era was no where near that advanced." The young Courier paused. "He could have killed me."

"But he didn't" Petric said. "Put it out of your mind and get on with the tour. We'll catch up with him later. In fact, I even know how we're going to do it. . . ."

Chapter Twenty-One
RICHMOND, VIRGINIA, APRIL 2, 1865

The tourists were gathered for Sunday service in St. Paul's Church. With the exception of the quiet murmur of the nearby river and the ringing of the church bells, the morning was peaceful. Marden had rejoined the group.

Rafe whispered, "The gaunt man in the private pew is Jefferson Davis, the President of the Confederacy. He is about to receive news that will change the face of the Confederate capitol forever."

A messenger approached Davis. Bending, he tapped the gaunt Davis on the arm, whispered to him, and slipped a piece of paper into his hand. With only a slight pallor to indicate his concern, Davis rose and walked from the church.

Rafe whispered, "A telegraphed message has just arrived from Lee, informing Davis that their positions must be abandoned tonight. The Confederate

lines have been crushed at Five Forks, and the city of
Richmond is no longer safe."

The tourists moved quickly outside. They watched
a large house where several government offices had
been set up across from the church. In the middle of
the street, piles of government documents were being
heaped and burned.

"It's not going to take long for word to spread.
Orders will go out for the trains to be readied for
Davis and his staff. Civilians will gather their belong-
ings and prepare to abandon their homes."

They traveled another three hours down the
line and saw the streets fill with baggage wagons,
carts, drays, and ambulances. The tourists were jos-
tled by crowds of people rushing through the streets.

"Where are they all going?" Margot Stuart asked.

Rafe shook his head. "The Danville depot, the
Fredricksburg depot, the houses of family and friends
who live far enough away from the capital for them
to feel safe from the invasion of the 'dread Yankees.'"

Rafe picked up the pace of the tour. They came
to the periphery of a great gathering, and Rafe saw
that a commissary store had opened its doors to the
public and was distributing previously hoarded goods.
Women, children, and wounded and able-bodied men
pressed forward, their arms raised and their hands
open, desperate for what they could carry. Huge
hams and bags of flour and sugar were dragged away.

Rafe shouted, "We're going to the station!"

They shunted up the line to a peaceful time,
several weeks earlier, and found transportation to
the Danville station. Rafe asked the driver of their

four-horse wagon to stop at Ninth Street. The driver shrugged and complied.

The tourists stepped out of the wagon, and Rafe said, "I want you to have an idea why we're not going to spend a lot of time on the streets."

At the same moment their driver looked away long enough to light a cigar, the group vanished.

Night slammed down. It was seven o'clock, and bonfires burned up and down the street. By their flickering light, the tourists saw Confederate soldiers looting Antoni's confectionery, eagerly taking all the candy they could get their hands on. Civilians had broken into a half-dozen other businesses, including a jewelry store. A riot was breaking out.

Petric shunted them back. They arrived seconds after they had left.

The tourists climbed back into the wagon, and they finished their journey to the Danville station. Although the cars were busy, the scene was tranquil compared to what they would soon face.

"By six P.M. on April second, close to half a million dollars in gold and silver bullion was secured on the cars: this was the fortune of the Confederacy. Everyone, stay close."

Rafe looked at Petric. The Patrolman nodded slightly, and they shunted back to the madhouse of people evacuating Richmond. The trains were literally crawling with desperate humanity. People were crushed up against the windows of the carriages, and hundreds of men swarmed on top of the cars, on the platforms, on the engines—anywhere they could find a handhold.

Midshipmen kept anyone else from getting close to the trains, insisting that they show a pass from the Secretary of War. Some of the boys were as young as twelve years old. A black-haired, red-faced major stalked back and forth.

The major, Daniel Williamson, was Rafe's ancestor. A trunk containing this man's personal effects inspired Rafe's interest, then obsession, with the era of the Civil War. According to history, Major Williamson would survive the war, marry his somewhat younger sweetheart, and raise a family with her, thus securing Rafe's lineage. If the major were to die during the evacuation of Richmond, all of Rafe's ancestors who came after the major would cease to exist, and so would Rafe.

The lives of both Rafe and his adversary seemed to be intertwined in some mysterious way that Rafe had yet to fathom. If you separated them, their enemy might show himself—if it didn't kill Rafe first.

The plan was to attempt to kill Rafe's ancestor. It was very likely that the disguised assailant would be somewhere in the crowd. They hoped that their actions would force the man to show himself and try to stop them. Petric had already vowed that, if they were successful in killing the major, he would go back in time and prevent them from going through with it.

"I'm not sure I can do this," Rafe said to the Patrolman.

"I'm not going to give you any choice." Petric removed his compression pack. Sliding the shiny sensor plate back, he revealed an obsidian square with a red thumb print painted on its surface. He pressed his thumb on the black surface.

"Activated," a metallic voice called out. "At the beep, you will have fifty-nine seconds to clear the blast area."

The Patrolman was about to slip the compression pack in the back pocket of the major when a high, piercing scream came from one of the tourists.

The young Courier spun and saw the man who had attacked him with a razor the day before holding Denise from behind. One arm was around her throat. The single-shot Remington was pressed into her ribs.

She could smell lilac as she cried out, "Rafe, help me!"

"Tell the Patrolman to get away from Major Williamson," the man without eyebrows said. "And tell him to put his little toy back in his pocket."

Petric didn't move. The device was still in his hand.

"Forty-five seconds," the pack said in an urgent but polite tone.

The rest of the tourists huddled behind Dewey. Jack and Margot clung to each other. Chuck stood beside them, slack jawed. Kyla held on to Tarrant, who managed to smile despite his fear.

The crowds around them barely noticed the hostage scene being played out. The major and two of the midshipmen ordered the gunman to put his weapon down. The assailant merely grinned and looked back to Rafe.

"Funny, you don't look a thing like him, even if he is your ancestor. But you both love to give orders.

Did you really think I'd let you kill your own ancestor, just to break the chain of events?"

No, Rafe thought. *We were counting on the fact that you wouldn't.*

Petric looked at the gunman and smiled. "You've got to admit, we flushed you out."

"Thirty seconds," the device said.

"Give it to me," Rafe said.

"It's your funeral," the Patrolman replied. He tossed the bomb to Rafe.

"I'm the one you're after," Rafe said evenly. "Let her go."

The gunman tightened his grip on Denise. A single tear rolled down Denise's face.

"Why are you doing this?" Rafe said. "Why are you trying to set me up?"

A look of intense hatred crossed the gunman's face. "You'll find out. You took something from me. Now I'm going to take something from you."

The gunman noticed the Patrolman's absence. "Where—"

Suddenly Petric appeared behind the assailant. He'd shunted to the past, circled to where the gunman would be standing, then shunted to the present time. He took a quick step forward, knocking the gun up into the air. The weapon fired harmlessly.

"Single shot," Petric snarled. "Stupid!"

Denise drove her elbow into the gunman's stomach and twisted out of his grip. With his free hand, Petric reached under the gunman's vest and tore open the thin plastic of his Time Belt. It sagged forward, but the man without eyebrows had hooked the device through the belt loops of his trousers. He grabbed for his timer.

"Don't!" Petric said, He leaped forward.

The gunman vanished.

It took everyone a moment to wonder why they hadn't been blown to bits.

"Okay, I lied," Petric said. "My pocket computer just did what I told it to do and say."

Rafe went to Denise and threw his arms around her. "I never thought he'd go for you. I'm so sorry."

She held him close.

Major Williamson pushed forward through the crowd. Petric snatched the single-shot Remington from the floor and shunted the group down the line.

Chapter Twenty-Two

In the parlor of a small house on Richmond's West Main Street, the tourists had come to join a small crowd which had gathered to witness the wedding of Colonel Walter Taylor and Elizabeth Saunders. Outside, the city was burning. Inside, as Dr. Minnigerode pronounced the couple man and wife, the only flames came from the flickering candles.

Rafe and Denise held hands as the bride and groom kissed. Feeling brave, Tarrant put his arm around Kyla, who was staring at Rafe and Denise. Kyla wriggled free and gave him a look of scorn.

"What?" Tarrant asked.

Then she caught Rafe glancing in their direction and raised an eyebrow. Without turning away, she reached over, grabbed a handful of Tarrant's shirt, yanked the boy toward her, and kissed him full on the lips. He was trembling as she let him go. In her best Southern Belle voice, she said, "You see, that's not *gentlemanly* behavior."

Stuck for a reply, Tarrant said, "Huh?"

Rafe led Denise to the rear of the party and motioned for the other tourists to follow. Leaving the Crenshaw home felt like stepping out of an airlock. The warmth, love, and calm suddenly disappeared, replaced by the cold night air and the madness that could be seen and heard erupting down the block.

"Why did you have Petric bring us here?" Denise asked.

Rafe had been drawn to the wedding by an urge to see love and commitment triumph over chaos and fear, but he couldn't find the words to express it.

"I just wanted to share this with you."

Turning to Petric, Rafe said, "Last stop. Ten A.M. Monday morning."

The Patrolman took them down the line.

Blinding sunlight greeted them. The fires on the horizon had worsened, filling the air with a dense black smoke, and shells continued to explode near the arsenal. Columns of incoming Union soldiers marched through the streets. The blacks of the city, who had been quietly observant, now cheered and surged forward to greet the black regiments riding through to the capital. Dozens of black soldiers rose up in their stirrups, waving their sabres and shouting. Women curtsied as children waved small Union flags. The drum corps played "Battle Cry of Freedom."

Rafe allowed the tourists to enjoy the spectacle and celebration for a time, then signaled Petric to take the group up the line to three weeks before.

Suddenly the streets were peaceful and quiet. The tourists walked a few blocks until they found a horse carriage. It delivered them to the Danville depot in time to take the evening train to Appomattox Station.

It was very late when they arrived at Appomattox. They made their way through the quiet little village and found the two-story brick McClean House, with its large, open porch and wide inviting steps.

"The owner of this house, Wilmer McClean, came two hundred miles just to avoid ever seeing another soldier after his land and his home were ruined in the conflict. McClean certainly never expected to throw his doors open to Grant and Lee for their discussion of the terms of surrender for the Confederate army, and he wasn't happy to do so. His fence rails were wrecked, his crops trampled, his home once again overrun. Lee surrendered, on Palm Sunday, April ninth, 1865."

Petric took his cue and shunted the group down the line to the early afternoon of April ninth. Suddenly they were engulfed by a crowd of soldiers and civilians who were making way for General Lee and General Grant, who were walking from a nearby apple tree. Robert E. Lee wore a new uniform, a bright yellow sash, gold spurs, and shiny new boots decorated with red silk. The dark uniform Grant wore was filthy. The leader of the Confederate army accepted his defeat with dignity, and the Federal soldiers greeted him with utmost respect.

After Grant and Lee signed the agreement, Rafe and Petric brought the tourists back up the line to the same quiet evening when they had first arrived.

Rafe led them from the house and back to the station.

On the ride back to Washington, Rafe was surprised to find Petric and Margot Stuart spending time together. Sometime later, Rafe got the Patrolman alone and said, "There's something I wanted to ask you about. I know it's not any of my business, but you're married, and Margot's married, and—"

"Think," Petric said coldly. "Why am I here?"

"To find out who's behind the forgeries," Rafe said automatically.

"Don't you remember what happened just before we left on the tour? Kyla and her mother were *drenched* in Charanea XII."

"The perfume you smelled on the wrapping paper that Whistler's painting arrived in," Rafe said.

Marden was sitting near the front of the carriage, staring at his hands. Chuck Stuart and Dewey were in the opposite seat. Rafe sat down beside the historian, who did not look up.

"William," Rafe said, "we need to talk. I know you're angry about what happened in Washington last time, but what we did was necessary."

"I'm not angry," Marden said incredulously. "I'm ashamed." He turned to Rafe, his lips trembling, his skin pale. "I've spent my entire life studying the past, revering what has gone before. From what you showed me, I made a mockery of all I believe in. When we go back, I'm terminating my work at the university. I don't belong there anymore."

"I think you do," Rafe insisted. "All right, I'll admit coming into the living past like this isn't for everyone. But we need people like you on the other side, putting all our findings in perspective for the people who will never have the chance to come up the line and experience it for themselves. What you do in now-time is more important than you realize."

The historian thought it over. "But won't I be facing charges for timecrimes?"

"No," Rafe said. "That's been taken care of, providing nothing else happens."

"You don't think I would do it again, do you?"

"William, there's only one stop left on this tour."

With a grave expression, Marden nodded and said, "April fourteenth. That awful Friday."

"We have tickets for the evening presentation of *Our American Cousin*. At ten after ten that evening, John Wilkes Booth enters the theater and shoots Mr. Lincoln. Before we get off the train, I need to know if you plan on attending."

Marden's eyes became wide. "You would take that risk?"

"It's better than having you punish yourself for the rest of your life."

"He's right," Dewey said unexpectedly. "Everyone makes mistakes. The past can be dangerous for any of us. Especially your first time. Believe me, I know."

Rafe couldn't believe what he was hearing. Apparently, neither could Marden.

"You think I can do this?" Marden asked, his voice shaky. "To see the President has always been my dream."

"Everyone should have a chance at their dreams," Dewey said. "No matter what they've done."

Rafe turned back to Marden. "Think about whether or not you can live with what's going to happen. I've been there before. It's not easy to sit through, not for someone with your love for the President. You can give me your decision when we reach the station."

"No," Marden said. "I'll tell you now. I solemnly pledge to attend the performance and to do nothing to alter the outcome. You have my word as a historian."

"That's all I need," Rafe said. He rose and started back to his seat.

Chapter Twenty-Three

After checking in at the Willard Hotel, Rafe took the group on a brief tour of the city. They spent an hour in an exclusive shop on Pennsylvania Avenue, where Margot, Kyla, and Denise purchased bonnets that were customized on the spot. Then they journeyed to the National Hotel, where Rafe had Petric shunt the group to just after 9:00 A.M on April fourteenth. They waited in the lobby for their first glimpse of the man who would kill the President.

"Remember," Rafe said, "Booth is to this era what Chaplin, Redford, and Dennison were to theirs. It's not unusual for people to stare at him, or to compliment him on a performance or a certain role."

A few minutes later, a man with slick black hair, a full mustache, piercing eyes and smooth, powdered skin arrived fresh from the barbershop. This was John Wilkes Booth. As he checked with the clerk at the front desk for his mail, Booth noticed the intense stares and forced smiles he was receiving from the tourists.

"Yes?" he said politely.

Before Rafe could say anything, William Marden surged forward and said, "Mr. John Wilkes Booth?"

"Yes, that is so."

The gaunt man smiled broadly. "May I be so bold, sir, as to ask for your autograph?"

"Oh. Of course, of course," Booth scribbled a quick autograph and handed the envelope back. "A pleasant morning to you and your friends."

Marden returned to the other tourists. They gathered round and stared at the inscription: "To William Marden, with hope that your name shall endure as long as mine. John Wilkes Booth."

"Of course I wanted to kill him," Marden said when they were back on the street. "But I *am* a historian. And the sanctity of now-time must be preserved."

Rafe led the group to Taltavul's saloon, just east of the Ford Theater. He and Petric had met their disguised assailant in this saloon in the alternate 1865 that Marden had created. At the end of the crowded bar, three men sat enjoying their drinks.

Rafe pointed to the thirty-four-year-old sandy-haired man in the middle.

"John F. Parker. The personal guard assigned by the police to Lincoln. Parker should be sitting in front of the door leading to the President's box. Instead he decided he wanted to see the play. When he tired of that, he came here to have a few drinks with Burns, the coachman, and Forbes, the valet. Look who else had the same idea."

Booth entered the saloon and ordered a bottle of whiskey with some water. Another man raised his glass to the actor and said, "You'll never be the actor your father was."

The actor smiled and said, "When I leave the stage, I will be the most famous man in America."

Through it all, Parker and his companions remained oblivious.

"They had no idea what Booth was up to!" Jack Stuart said in amazement.

"It's time to take in the performance," Rafe said.

Leading the tourists into the theater, Rafe presented the tickets. As the group was ushered inside, Jack Stuart asked, "Aren't we going to wait outside to see Lincoln?"

"The President doesn't arrive until Act One has already begun," Rafe assured the man.

As the group entered a dark corridor, Petric hit the timer. There was no perceivable difference in their surroundings; the tourists didn't even know that they had shunted up the line a month into the past. It was now a cold March evening, and the play they were about to see was not *Our American Cousin*. It was *The Apostate*.

There was also a cast change that Rafe hoped would startle one of the tourists into giving himself away.

The gas-lit theater seated seventeen hundred people. The curving rows of chairs spread out from the center. A double stairway led off from the lobby to the dress circle and the upper boxes.

The President's box, draped with Union flags, was set up on the right side of the stage. A rail surrounded it. The tourists sat together, filling out a cluster of seats in the front three rows of the parquet. It wasn't long before the theater was packed and the President and his first lady took their seats. Gripping the rail, Lincoln waved to the crowd.

Marden shook his head and said, "This isn't right. Miss Harris and Major Rathbone are supposed to be in attendance with Mr. Lincoln."

"Sit back and enjoy the show," Rafe hissed. "Don't say another word."

Ashen faced, the historian nodded. The applause died down, and the play began.

It wasn't long before the villain of the play was introduced. Despite himself, Rafe felt outrage well up in his heart as the twenty-six-year-old actor took the stage.

John Wilkes Booth commanded the audience.

From the sharp intake of breath beside him, Rafe knew that Marden had recognized the actor, too. As casually as he could, Rafe looked at the other tourists. They were all confused by Booth's presence on stage, but not one of them betrayed himself.

Twice during the play, John Wilkes Booth stormed toward the President, directing threatening lines of dialogue at the great man, even thrusting his finger at Lincoln's face.

It wasn't until the intermission that Rafe explained what was going on. Mrs. Lincoln had invited

Mary Clay and her sister, Sallie, to an evening at the theater. Mr. Nicolay and John Hay served as their escorts.

"Very few people realize that Booth had come this close to the President only a month before the assassination. Booth was a star in his time, making as much as twenty thousand dollars a year. Now, everyone follow me. We're going back to April fourteenth, where we'll see Lincoln arrive. And following him is a tragedy that will darken the mood of a nation."

Unnoticed by Rafe, an old man was selling flowers in the lobby. He had a surplus of lilacs. By the time the tourists had left, the old man had one less.

Chapter Twenty-Four

WASHINGTON, D.C.,
APRIL 14, 1865

Rafe had hoped that the assailant would follow the group to the earlier event and strike there. The delicate web of events during the assassination could not be interfered with, although Rafe wished in his heart that they could be. Petric stood beside Rafe and whispered, "We tried."

Tonight Lincoln would be seated in the upper box, sixteen feet above the stage. The tourists were in the dress circle, the only seats with a view into the box.

8:00 P.M. arrived. The hiss of the gaslights quieted, the theater darkened, and the curtains parted.

At twenty-five minutes after the hour, Rafe cautioned the tourists that Lincoln would soon arrive. Within minutes, footsteps issued from the winding stairway.

"The President," Rafe whispered, and the tourists looked to the rear of the dress circle in time to

see Lincoln, his wife, and another couple walk behind the back row of chairs. A standing ovation
began in the dress circle.

In seconds the entire audience was on its feet,
and the orchestra struck up "Hail to the Chief."

In the dress circle, Petric sniffed once more,
rather loudly, and his eyes suddenly lit up. "That's
it," he said excitedly. *"That's it."*

Rafe looked at the Patrolman curiously.

As the applause died and the patrons began to
sit down, the Patrolman ordered the tourists from
their seats and conducted them toward the darkened
hallway to the rear. Once they were safely hidden
from curious stares, Petric ushered the group toward
the stairs and said, "We're leaving."

Jack Stuart said, "But Lincoln won't be assassi-
nated until ten after ten. We'll miss the whole thing!"

"Can't be helped," Petric said curtly.

They were at the top of the stairs when a voice
called out from behind them. "You're not going
anywhere."

Rafe spun and saw the gunman, who had gone
back to his first weapon of choice: the silent pulse
rifle. He was dressed in an elegant black suit, but his
face—scars, no eyebrows—was the same as it had
been on the train. The gunman focused his attention
on Petric. "So, you know who I am?"

"The height almost fooled me," Petric said. "But
the lilac gave you—"

The gunman squeezed the trigger. The Patrolman was lifted from his feet by the blast, the impact
slamming him into the wall. Then he slumped to the

floor; his face was turned away from the tourists. Smoke rose from the back of his jacket.

It was too much for Rafe to take in at once. He had been wrong about Petric. The gunman swung to the pulse rifle toward Rafe's chest and smiled as he said, "Now you. I've waited a long time for this."

Kyla took a few steps forward and crossed her arms as she looked at Petric. "That's *disgusting*."

The sound of her voice drew the gunman's attention. His hateful glare faded for an instant. Kyla's expression changed into one of startled recognition as she saw his face and allowed her hand to touch the purple lilac that had been attached to her dress like a corsage.

Instinctively, the young Courier reached for the timer strapped to his waist, Dewey's timer, on a useless tourist's Time Belt. Another figure suddenly winked into existence beside the fallen Patrolman just as Rafe punched the timer at his waist.

To his absolute amazement, Rafe shunted.

Chapter Twenty-Five

Rafe's first impression was that he was standing on the edge of an abyss, about to topple backward into endless darkness. He fought for a moment to regain his balance, then took a few steps forward and pressed his hands against the wall he hadn't even realized was there. Rafe's vision adjusted to the darkness, and he tried to get his bearings. Turning carefully, he pressed against the wall and looked out at a great, yawning pit before him.

It was almost twilight. Rafe was standing in the same corridor on the second floor of the theater. The ruined stairs were before him, exposed at their right flank and leading down into the aftermath of a tragedy. As he studied the wreckage below, Rafe saw that much of the second floor had collapsed.

Rafe had more pressing concerns. Dewey's belt was not supposed to be a Master Belt, but it had functioned as one. That meant the instructor had lied. If he actually believed Rafe was a criminal, he would never had supplied the Courier with the means to escape at any time. His silence meant that he wanted to cover up the fact that he was wearing a Master Belt.

Just as the true criminal would have to be.

The young Courier heard a noise behind him and turned. The gunman was staring at him in shock. The man still held his pulse rifle.

Rafe knew he had only a few seconds. Moving faster than he ever had in his life, Rafe kicked the rifle out of the other man's hands. It fired three staccato bursts that ripped across the ceiling. The rifle hit the edge of the floor, teetered for a moment, then fell ten meters to the ground.

Rafe had allowed himself to become momentarily distracted by the gun and its destination. He was caught by surprise when the man lunged at him. Powerful hands closed on Rafe's throat as he and the man were carried over the top of the stairs. Rafe hit hard, and the wooden edge of the third step drove itself into his back. An explosion of pain engulfed his senses.

Reacting with animal instinct, Rafe flung his arms open and tried to arrest his fall. The fingers of his right hand closed over a half-exposed support beam, then his left foot punched through a rotted piece of railing and hooked on a chunk of concrete that refused to give.

The gunman still gripped Rafe's throat. The Courier brought his right leg up and kicked as hard as he could. The man was flung over Rafe toward the winding stairs beyond. Rafe heard the gunman's body strike the stairs, tumble a few times, then stop. Using the holds he had found, Rafe pulled himself up to the top landing. When he turned and looked down the stairs, he was surprised to see the gunman dragging himself to his feet. The man moved as though injured, but his anger appeared great enough to force him on.

Rafe knew that there was enough time to escape. His hands went to his timer, then stopped.

No, he thought. *This ends. Here and now.*

Taking his compression pack and expanding it to full size, Rafe withdrew the item Petric had entrusted to him, the single-shot Remington. The gun had been loaded with a lead ball nearly three centimeters in circumference. A percussion cap had been placed under the hammer. It was ready to fire.

The gunman appeared at the top of the stairs. Rafe aimed the small, brass gun. The man laughed. His hand was already on his belt.

"I could be gone in an instant. You'll never find me. But I can always find you. And your little girlfriend."

Rafe fired. There was a shower of sparks as the man's timer exploded. The force of the impact spun the man around. He screamed and held his wounded, bloodied hand before his face. The ruined timer on his Time Belt crackled and sparked, but the man was wearing Kevlar and his stomach had been protected.

A cloud of smoke enveloped Rafe, then quickly cleared. Before him, the gunman was laughing. "You better run while you can," he said. "Single-shot weapon. Stupid. Remember?"

"Why are you doing this?" Rafe demanded, staring at the man's darkened features. "I don't even know you."

"You know me. And I told you why before. You took something from me. This is payback."

Despite the smoke, Rafe could smell the scent of lilac as the man advanced and took a rough but ferocious swing at him. As Rafe darted out of the way he felt a burst of pain like liquid fire rush along his back. He had been injured, too. "We're too close to the ledge," Rafe said.

The man didn't care. He swung again, quicker than Rafe expected. The blow caught Rafe squarely in the face and sent him staggering backward. *The ledge,* he thought. *Where is it?*

The gunman surged forward, favoring his wounded hand. He tried to deliver an open-handed blow to the side of Rafe's head.

Grabbing the gunman's wounded hand, he squeezed. The gunman threw back his head and howled in pain. Rafe twisted, felt an incredible pain in his back, and heaved the gunman off. The man rolled twice, came to the edge of the shattered floor, and stopped. He was trembling, about to pick himself up for another attack, when the section of ledge beneath him crumbled. Screaming, he fell to the ground below.

Rafe reached for his timer, then stopped. He couldn't just leave the gunman.

Crawling to the top of the stairs, Rafe carefully hobbled down to the landing and found the spot where the man had fallen. He was unconscious but alive. He had broken his leg in the fall.

Rafe heard the sounds of children from somewhere close. Forcing himself to go on despite the white-hot pain coursing through his entire body, Rafe found the front door, unlocked it from the inside, and called out to one of three young boys who were playing in front of the theater.

"The time," he said hoarsely. "I need to know the date and the time."

They told him.

Chapter Twenty-Six

When Rafe materialized in front of his tourists, only a few seconds had elapsed for them. He was afraid that the earlier version of the gunman would still be there, but the gunman had already shunted down the line, frightened off by a tall, well-armed Patrolman, who was now bending over Petric.

Denise barely restrained a scream when she saw Rafe. The others turned as she ran to him. He collapsed in her arms, and she helped him to the floor.

The Patrolman left Petric's side and said, "Are you all right, son?"

Rafe was stunned when he looked at the Patrolman. In seconds he put a name to the face.

"Coffin," Rafe said. The last time he had seen George Coffin was at Chancellorsville. The Patrolman had tried to save Stonewall Jackson's life.

"It's complicated," Coffin said. "We'll explain it all later."

Rafe nodded. "I got the man who did this. I can lead you to him, once we get everyone back to now-time."

Kyla sighed. "Rafe, you're so brave. I hope you'll let me do something *special* for you when we get back."

Denise shook her head at the girl's absurd performance.

But someone else took her very seriously. "What about me?" Tarrant asked in a quiet voice. "I thought you were my girl."

"Don't be an idiot," Kyla said. "The only reason I let you near me was to make Rafe jealous. I should have known he wouldn't consider a runt like you serious competition."

"That's not true," Tarrant said, tears welling up in his eyes. "You liked me. You said so."

He turned to Rafe, a familiar look of hatred marring his features. "It's all your fault! I hate you!"

Kyla frowned. "Don't pay him any attention. No one else does."

Tarrant backed away.

"Where's Dewey?" Rafe asked.

"He ran off after your friend with the pulse rifle shunted out," Coffin said. "Don't worry. Another Patrolman picked him up the second he left the theater."

"Then you knew he was part of the forgery scheme."

"We suspected," Coffin said. "We can go over this later. Right now—"

"Wait," Rafe said. He pointed at the beautiful

purple lilac attached to Kyla's dress. "Where did you get that?"

Kyla shrugged. "Tarrant gave it to me."

Suddenly Margot called out, "What's that awful child doing?"

They all turned to see Tarrant stripping the Master Belt from Petric. Before anyone could move to stop him, Tarrant hit the belt's timer and vanished.

"Why didn't you stop him?" Rafe demanded.

"We weren't meant to. The disruption to the timestream would have been too great." Coffin rose and reset his timer for now-time. He wore a Master Belt, and it had already been keyed to control all the tourist's belts. The Patrolman gave Rafe the proper numbers to key into his own timer.

"I'll do it," Denise said.

Kyla cleared her throat and saw Rafe staring at the lilac. She pulled it off and handed it to him, then went back to her parents. As he smelled the flower's fragrance, the meaning of the gunman's words became clear.

"It was him," Rafe said as they prepared to shunt. "It was Tarrant all along."

Coffin was about to touch the master control timer when Rafe turned to his charges. "We have a tour to complete."

"Are you sure?" Coffin said.

Rafe nodded. The Patrolman reset his timer and took Petric down the line. Denise and Marden helped Rafe back into the theater, where they took their seats with the other tourists and watched the play.

Shortly after 10:00 P.M., Mrs. Mountchessington

learned that Asa was not wealthy at all. In horror she
said, "No heir to the fortune, Mr. Trenchard?"

"Oh, no," Asa replied.

Young Augusta was also stunned. "What! No
fortune!"

"Nary a red," he said cheerfully. "It all comes
from barking up the wrong tree about the old man's
property."

Rafe glanced to the President's box. Lincoln was
all but hidden by the draperies, but his silhouette
could be seen rocking back and forth.

Mrs. Mountchessington said, "Augusta, to your
room!"

"Yes, Ma. The nasty beast!" The actress made
her exit.

"I am aware, Mr. Trenchard, that you are not
used to the manners of good society," Mrs. Mountchessington said as she stormed off the stage in a
huff, leaving Asa alone.

"Don't know the manners of good society, eh?
Wal, I guess I know enough to turn you inside out,
you sockdolgizing old mantrap!"

Buried amidst the laughter—the reason Booth
had picked this particular moment to strike—came
the sound of a gunshot. The tourists looked to the
President's box in time to see the President's head
sink to his chest. The rocking had stopped.

In the box, a cloud of smoke had enveloped
Booth. Quite calmly he said, *"Sic semper tyrannis!"*
It was the motto of Virginia: "Thus be it ever to
tyrants." Booth forced his way between the mortally
wounded President and his first lady, whose laughter

had given way to confusion. Major Rathbone, un-
aware of what was going on, rose and grappled with
Booth. The actor drew a knife and stabbed the major, then shoved the major away and boldly called
out, "Revenge for the South!"

A scream pierced the theater from the President's box. It was Mary Todd Lincoln. From the
orchestra seats, Major Joseph P. Stewart cried, "Stop
that man!" Mrs. Lincoln screamed again. The audience was now alive with the sounds of dread. There
were cries for water from the State box.

"For God's sake, what is it? What happened?"
someone called out.

From the box, a man cried, "He has shot the
President!"

In the dress circle, the tourists were quiet, as
stunned as the audience. It was a moment none of
them would ever forget. Booth had already made
good his escape, but he would not be free long.
Eleven days later, while running from the burning
barn on Garrett's farm, Booth would be shot in the
back of the head by Sergeant Boston Corbett. As he
lay dying, Booth would stare at his hands and mut-
ter, "Useless! Useless!"

"Let me get this straight," Rafe said. "This whole thing was a setup from the beginning?"

The young Courier was sitting in the office of Ivan Pendergrass. Coffin and Petric sat beside him. Pendergrass was wearing a Viking helmet, a dark-aquamarine tee-shirt, a leather jacket, and mirrored sunglasses. One of his front teeth had been capped with gold. It glimmered when he smiled.

Pendergrass said, "We were hoping it would draw someone out. When Dewey insisted on going on this tour, on seeing justice done, we were naturally suspicious. Especially considering what happened to him the last time he went up the line, at the start of his career."

"I don't know anything about that," Rafe said.

"Nor should you," Petric said, breaking in. "Dewey had trained to become a Courier. No one scored higher on the academic side than he did. But it was during his field training that it all went bad for him. He was apprenticed to Terrence Stiers, one of the best Couriers of his day. They were assigned to the Aztec run, Montezuma's battle against Cortez. Stiers's timer became defective, and they were captured. Dewey was faced with the choice of sacrificing either himself or Stiers and the tourists. He returned to now-time. They died horribly. Dewey heard it, saw it. Most of it, anyway."

"But Stiers is still alive," Rafe said. "I've met him."

"Of course," Pendergrass said. "The Patrol went back and saved them. No one but Dewey has memories of what happened. Those memories proved difficult to live with. After that, he was too unstable for the field."

"So he became an instructor," Rafe said.

"Correct. Until he became greedy, that is. Right now he's with interrogation, falling all over himself naming names. We should have all of his 'business partners' in custody by tomorrow."

"What about Tarrant?"

"That's a different matter entirely," Coffin said. "Although he was only fifteen when the tour left, he had already been the leader of his criminal 'empire' for over two years. What it comes down to is this: Tarrant wanted attention from his parents. Since he couldn't get that, he wanted money to get free of them. His own money. He came up with the entire scheme after he met Dewey by accident at the Under D.C. Museum. They became friends, then partners who were bonded together by their anger and frustration.

"You see, despite what had happened on his first tour, Dewey was embittered by his many lost opportunities to return to field duty, even though it was his own reluctance that caused him to be passed over."

"I still don't understand why you set me up," Rafe said. "Why didn't you tell me what was going on?"

"Your performance had to be utterly convincing," Pendergrass said. "If you didn't believe you were in serious trouble, the criminals wouldn't have believed it either."

"We were getting close to whoever was responsible," Petric said, "just as we had been several times before. But every time we got too close, the operation closed up and vanished. So we decided to put out some bait."

"Me," Rafe said.

"Yes. We had to manufacture a Courier in disgrace and spread the word so that our targets would find out about it. We believed that they would seize the opportunity to shift the attention away from themselves. After all, who's going to continue an investigation when the criminal has already been captured and sentenced? Tarrant knew it was too risky to do it all himself, so he forced Dewey to join the tour."

Rafe shook his head. "What happened to Tarrant after he escaped at the Ford? Young Tarrant, that is."

"He spent four years up and down the line,

committing crimes, cultivating his hatred of you, until he was finally ready to strike," Petric said.

"Because the Time Patrol was onto him," Rafe said.

"And because of Kyla. He had never been in love before. As far as he was concerned, you had taken her away from him. He wore the lilac because the scent reminded him of her, or the way he remembered her, anyway. Her perfume smelled of lilacs."

"I thought it was just another clue leading us to the Ford Theater," Rafe said.

"What do you mean?" Coffin said.

"Walt Whitman's famous poem about the death of Lincoln: 'When Lilacs Last in the Dooryard Bloom'd.'" Rafe shifted uncomfortably. "He knew how I felt about President Lincoln, and he knew the theater was the perfect place to strike. He had a single-shot Remington, just like Booth's and he pretended to be an actor, like Booth. Then the lilac . . . it all fit."

"No," Petric said. "It all came down to love."

Rafe looked at his twin reflections in Pendergrass's mirrored sunglasses. "I need a few minutes alone with you."

The huge man nodded. Petric and Coffin left.

"You used me," Rafe said.

"And I want to make it up to you," Pendergrass said. "Whatever you want, just name it."

"I want to go back to when Denise and I were together. I want to make it all right between us again."

Pendergrass took off the mirrored sunglasses.

His eyes were dark. "I can't let you do that."

"I know. So what I need is time to try to make it work between us now."

Pendergrass nodded. "Take all the time you need. That's one thing we've got plenty of."

The young Courier rose and went to the door. His back was turned, and when Pendergrass asked him to wait, Rafe didn't turn around. "Whatever you decide, Rafe, the Master Belt is yours. Just don't screw up time with it."

Surprised, Rafe turned.

But Pendergrass was gone.

Chapter Twenty-Eight
WASHINGTON, D.C., APRIL 9, 1865

The *River Queen* had docked, and President Lincoln and his wife had come home to the White House. Tomorrow, when news of Lee's surrender became public, the streets would be alive with celebration. But for the moment, Lincoln didn't know.

It had taken Rafe five trips up the line into the past to arrange for his audience with the President this evening. Now he stood before Lincoln, Denise at his side.

Just as Rafe was about to speak, Secretary of War Stanton burst into Lincoln's office with a telegraphic dispatch from General Grant.

His timing was perfect. Lincoln read the dispatch with trembling hands. He looked up in shock, afraid to believe what he had just read. Sensing the President's thoughts, Stanton said, "It's true!"

The two men threw their arms around each other. "Our prayers have been answered!" Lincoln cried, tears of joy streaming down his face. In that single moment, he seemed reborn. Rising, Lincoln walked to Rafe's side, clamped his strong hand on the young Courier's shoulder, and said, "If I have your assurance of silence until morning, I would share this wondrous news with you."

"Yes," Rafe said, "Of course!" Beside him, Denise nodded excitedly.

The fires of hope, love, and dreams for the future burned in the President's eyes. "General Lee surrendered the Army of Northern Virginia this morning. We will soon be a nation at peace again!"

Rafe congratulated the President, surrendering to tears of his own as Lincoln clasped Rafe's hand in both of his own.

"Your business here tonight. . . ." Lincoln prompted Rafe.

"It can wait, sir. We will call again another day."

Lincoln nodded, went to his desk, and scribbled a note that he gave to Rafe. "Show this when you return. I will see you at once. For now, you may stay for a time, enjoy the gardens if you would."

Rafe took a final look at the President's wide, joyous smile, then took Denise's hand and led her outside.

"That's how I'll always remember him," Rafe said. "I don't think I can ever come back again now. This moment is just too precious to ever part with."

"Then you've made up your mind," Denise said.

Gently cupping her face with his hands, Rafe said, "I know what's important to me."

As the sun faded in the sky, he leaned down and

kissed her full on the lips. She threw her arms around him, holding him tightly.

Above them, through his office window, the dark silhouette of the President paused for a moment, nodded approvingly at the young lovers, then turned away.

> *When lilacs last in the dooryard bloom'd,*
> *And the great star early droop'd in the western sky in the night,*
> *I mourn'd, and yet shall mourn, with ever returning spring.*
>
> —Walt Whitman

Afterword

We'll probably never know who history's first tourist was—the first person to take a long and difficult trip into an unfamiliar part of the world, not because he *had* to, but simply because he wanted to see what was there.

Some famous fictional travelers of antiquity come quickly to mind. The earliest of them is Gilgamesh, the hero of a group of epic poems composed in the Mesopotamian land of Sumer before 2000 B.C. There actually was a Gilgamesh—he was king of Uruk in Sumer about the year 2500 B.C.—but the epic poems, written long after his time, tell imaginary tales of his fantastic exploits. Searching for the secret of eternal life, Gilgamesh wandered far and wide and eventually came to the mysterious land of Dilmun, where he was able to obtain the plant called Grow-Young-Again (but he lost it on the way home).

To call Gilgamesh a "tourist," though, is hardly

accurate. He was, if anything, an explorer, pursuing a very specific goal, very much as Columbus was trying to find the Indies and Roald Amundsen to reach the South Pole. A tourist is motivated mainly by curiosity; and though Gilgamesh certainly was curious ("I am the pilgrim who has seen everything within the confines of the Land, and far beyond it," he says in the poem that bears his name) his travels were powered entirely by his hunger for immortality. If he had never become obsessed with eternal life, most likely he would have remained in the city of Uruk all his days.

Another celebrated fictional wanderer of ancient times was Sinuhe the Egyptian, whose travels come to us in an account set down on papyrus scrolls about 1200 B.C. Sinuhe, who supposedly lived about the time Tut-ankh-amen was pharaoh of Egypt, traveled to Syria, to Babylon, to Crete, and to many another land, and the tale of his wanderings makes for marvelously lively reading. But he too was no true tourist: he was an exile, driven out of his homeland beside the Nile by an angry king.

And then, of course, there was Odysseus of Ithaca, who spent ten years making his way back to Greece after the Torjan War, and whose adventures have maintained their fascination since Homer first told of them nearly three thousand years ago. But though he visited many an extraordinary place and saw many a marvel and wonder, Odysseus can no more be called a tourist than a hurricane can be called a strong breeze. He was a soldier trying to get home after fighting overseas, and his travels were

accidental detours on his way, not anything he would
have chosen to undergo.

I suspect that the real history of tourism begins
with Herodotus of Halicarnassus. No mythical char-
acter he; he was born in Asia Minor about 484 B.C.,
lived in Athens about the time Socrates and Plato
flourished there, and published a great work of history, which we still read with immense enjoyment,
some time between 431 and 425 B.C. His famous
book is ostensibly an account of the long war between Greece and Persia, but in order to provide
sufficient background material Herodotus delves into
all sorts of matters both true and legendary concern-
ing the entire ancient world, and so he produced a
wonderful and far-reaching tale filled with glorious
stories that have never lost their charm.

In the course of the studies that led up to his
book Herodotus traveled through much of the world
as it was known in his time—in Africa and Asia he
journeyed; in Egypt, up the Nile as far as Aswan, and
also to Libya, Syria, Babylonia, Lydia, Phrygia, and
Byzantium; and in the western world he went to
Thrace and Macedonia in what is now Greece, up
the Danube as far as modern-day Hungary or Austria,
and along the shores of the Black Sea into what has
become the Soviet Union. Wherever this incredibly
inquisitive man ventured, he gathered information
about local customs, religious beliefs, history: a great
reporter who was also a great storyteller.

Since Herodotus' time, tourism has become the
prime amusement of millions. In Europe a couple of
centuries ago it was common-place for aristocratic

young men to make the Grand Tour, traveling through neighboring countries in search of culture, fine food, and unusual experiences. The more hardy went on as Herodotus did into remote regions of Asia and Africa, coming back with discoveries that startled the world. But today such travel is not only the pastime of the wealthy: millions of people each year climb aboard jet planes that carry them away to spend a little time in some far-off place, be it Paris, London, or Timbuctoo. No region of Earth is completely free from such wanderers, not even Antarctica nor the slopes of Mount Everest. They can be seen everywhere, singly or in little groups, camera in one hand, guidebook in the other, eagerly taking in whatever sights there are to be seen. And, no doubt, the next century will see similar wide-eyed vacationers scurrying off for a first-hand look at the craters of the Moon, the dusty plains of Mars, and even, perhaps, the Great Red Spot of Jupiter.

Only one place seems safe from the sightseeing impulse so far—the past. We can read about it, we can daydream about it, we can dig up what is left of it and peer at the remains. But we can't get there from here.

Except, of course, by way of science fiction.

What a wonderful way to experience history the Time Tour would be! Instead of picking our way through the crumbling stones that are all that is left of the Roman Forum, we could don toga and sandals and move among the throngs as Caesar Augustus goes by in his chariot, or look on in wonder as the returning legions parade in triumph after yet another

victory in some far-off land. The Mexico of Moctezuma
would come alive in all its bloody beauty. We could
visit Kublai Khan's wondrous pleasure-dome in lost
Xanadu; we could buy choice seats at the Globe
Theater in London for the opening night of *Hamlet
or King Lear*, we could watch Pizarro's little army go
marching into Peru to conquer the mighty Incas. To
see Napoleon crown himself Emperor of France—to
watch Hector and Achilles fight it out before the
walls of Troy—to be on hand in Paris when Lind-
bergh's little plane reached the airport after its flight
across the Atlantic—how much more exciting that
would be than to read some historian's account, or
to see a few cracked bits of masonry, or to stand on
an Actual Historic Spot and stare at a plaque telling
us what once happened there. The great battles of
the past, the terrible assassinations, all the triumphs
and horrors of humanity's astonishing history, everything made available to us, safely and at a reasonable
price!

Well, so far it happens only in the imaginations
of science-fiction writers. But we can go on hoping. . . .

And when the era of Time Tours finally does
arrive, no doubt one of the most popular tours will
be the one to the American Civil War (though the
advertising brochures below the Mason-Dixon line
will call it the War Between the States.) This great
national calamity has exercised a powerful pull on the
American imagination for close to a century and a half,
now. Whole libraries of historical works have been
produced, analyzing every battle, every minor skirmish.
Such names as Fort Sumter, Bull Run, Antietam, Get-

tysburg, Harpers Ferry, Shiloh, and Chancellorsville
have taken a permanent place in our mythology. The
great leaders of the war years—Grant, Lee, Sherman,
McLellan, Beauregard, "Stonewall" Jackson, Jubal Early,
Jefferson Davis, above all Abraham Lincoln—live on
in our national memory with special vividness. Nov-
elists and film-makers have returned to the events of
the war again and again. It is all dreadfully real to us,
even now. And yet—if we could only see it actually
happen—

If only.

Time Tours, of course, will make it available,
everything from the early uncertain battles through
the grand moment of the Gettysburg Address to the
surrender of Lee's army. The trip will culminate with
that darkest and most tragic of events in our history,
the assassination of President Lincoln in the very
moment of triumph and national reunion.

When it does become possible for tourists to
sign up for trips to the past, though, a new kind of
vandalism will become a major problem: the attempts
of time travelers, well meaning or otherwise, to alter
events in human history. What a temptation it would
be to try to keep Lincoln from going to the theater
that fatal night—to bring back a few of the plays of
Sophocles that were lost when the library of Alexan-
dria burned—to warn the people of Pompeii that
Mount Vesuvius was about to erupt!

But any change in history must inevitably affect
the present-day world from which the time tourists
come from; and so the past must be kept sacred and
inviolate. Therefore we will need a Time Patrol. The

time travelers will have to be kept under close watch
to make certain that they don't succumb to the
temptation to make changes in the past, just as visi-
tors to museums and cathedrals are watched to keep
them from launching some sudden attack on a masterpiece of art.

Time must be avoided. And some very unlikely
people may turn out to be timecriminals. That's one
of the many tricky issues that Nick Baron considers
in his fine novel of tourists at the American Civil
War, *Glory's End.*

—Robert Silverberg

DATABANK

Time Services thoroughly researches a time period before opening it up to tourists. Research historians are sent back to study, map, photograph, tape, and record every aspect of life in a past era. Only when their work is finished do the Time Tours begin.

All hypnosleep courses for tourists (and couriers) are prepared based on fully accurate notes and recordings. Time Services is proud of its 99.98% accuracy rate in charting past events.

Before you take your Glory Road tour of the American Civil War, you may want to view events such as PICKETT'S CHARGE on your DESK HOLO. Pay attention to GUNS and other weapons of the era; remember, this is a military conflict.

Be sure to report to the TIME TOURS TRAVEL STATION promptly, and be sure that everything you bring into the past has been approved by your Time Courier. Good luck with your trip!

Time Tours Travel Station: Washington, D. C.

The Washington, D. C. Time Tour Travel Station is located within sight of the Capitol Building. Travel Pods, which use an underground rail system, provide fast transport to other cities.

The Desk Halo

Helpful to the Time Courier planning a tour, this device produces miniature holograms of historic events. Here, Denise and Rafe look at a hologram of the battle at Gettysburg.

The Hoverfloat and Ferrybot

The tourists of the Glory Road tour take a break from the bumpy trains of the Civil War Era. They are in now-time, and are boarding the silver hoverfloat. The ferrybot awaits payment. Rafe's thumbprint will authorize the group's entry.

A Travel Pod

Travel Pods are used for rapid transportation all over the world. They are miniature "bullet trains" that travel across a form of railway tracks using magnetic fields for propulsion. Pods are comfortable, affordable, and convenient.

Pickett's Charge

General Robert E. Lee suffered heavy losses in the battle of Gettysburg. On July 3, 1863, he gathered 15,000 men and mounted a major offensive: Pickett's Charge.